Crossing Rubicon

By

AJ BLANC

White-Knight Press

Crossing Rubicon is a work of fiction. Although there are <u>some</u> historical facts regarding places and events presented in this book, they are only provided to add a sense of realism to the overall narrative. All other names, places, characters and incidents portrayed in this book are the product of the author's imagination.

Library of Congress Control Number: 2019904278

Print ISBN	978-0-9994574-2-9
Ebook ISBN	978-0-9994574-3-6

Written and published in the United States of America

Dramatis Personae

Sonya Kane: Chief Hunter, former Marine Scout Sniper

Milo Durron: Deputy US Marshal, retired Army Master Sergeant

Jamey Kirlan: Supervisory Deputy US Marshal

Colonel Takbrite: US Army Criminal Investigation Division Commanding Officer

Jacen Carter: US Army Sergeant

William Karrde: US Army Criminal Investigation Division Agent

Jaina Isard: Daughter of US Air Force General Joben Isard

Marcus Hyde: US Air Force Senior Airman - Colonial Response Force

Darius Parker: US Marine Recon Corporal

Elad McCone: Hunter, former Governors Police Bureau Lieutenant

Joram Bachman: Rosen Network Lead Public Relations Announcer

Raymus Watson: Military Intelligence Contractor, former Navy SEAL

Alena Sarne: National Institute of Corrections Supervisor

Prologue: The World's a Stage
2076 - Zone Neptune

Another seeker drone fell from the sky. Its black and tan form tumbled across the bright Nevada sand only a few meters away from the man who shot it down. He quickly, yet meticulously, scanned the area with his specially designed rifle scope for any more unwanted visitors, and decided to risk leaving the cover of an abandoned utility shed after determining the area was clear. He eased out of the crumbling door frame, took one more look at his surroundings, and then sprinted toward the remains of a tank, long since overgrown with weeds. He dove into tufts of long grass and crawled under the rusting armored treads.

Peering out of a hole in the armor, made larger by decades of rust, he looked around at the other derelict military vehicles slowly decaying in the grassy depression of the landscape. Many of the machines that still had some semblance of a shape were familiar to him. He had even used a few of them while in the Army. When they were transported to this desolate place in Nevada however, their days were numbered. What eventually became referred to as Zone Neptune used to be where the Air Force tested its bombs and missiles on various vehicles, as well as experimental building materials.

The man, a contestant publicly known as Prisoner 24601, waited and listened. His number, while randomly chosen by the network, was quickly recognized as the prison number of the legendary Jean Valjean from Victor Hugo's *Les Misérables*, so the name Jean soon became a replacement for the number in the public eye. Ironically, Jean's alleged crimes weren't much more heinous than his fictional characters' namesake. Hugo's Jean was sent to prison for stealing bread; the retired Army Special Forces Jean was forced to choose between imprisonment for stealing life-saving medication for his wife, or participate in one of the Rosen Network's infamous game shows. He never would've guessed the show he would be placed into would be The Most Dangerous Game, a nefarious sporting event where trained 'hunters' track and kill convicted criminals, unless the hunted became the hunter.

With the promise of his wife getting the medicine she needed, Jean decided to take the plea deal and sign with Rosen. Ever the eternal optimist, he felt fortunate for being assigned to operate in the former military proving ground known as Zone Neptune, with its ample protection and supply drops. His respite, however, was broken when he heard the sound of a Cirrus X7 rocket pack power down nearby. Jean now knew his contender had finally tracked him down, but he dared not move and give away his position.

"Shooting seekers still provides a general location, which is why you haven't used yours, I suspect," the Chief Hunter yelled into the small valley of decaying war machines.

Jean knew the voice well. The first woman in the Marine Scout Sniper Division to have a confirmed kill count in the triple digits is difficult to forget. He knew it wouldn't take her long to find him, so he snaked his way into a position where he anticipated she'd approach. Jean selected smart targeting on his Heckler & Koch G11 rifle and waited tensely.

The late afternoon sun aided his efforts, casting her growing shadow onto the dilapidated shack he'd just vacated. The shadow materialized into an expertly camouflaged figure. The built-in scope on the revived weapons platform indicated his smart targeting was active, and he fired.

The caseless uranium core round punched through the rocket pack and into her left shoulder. Instinctively, and seemingly faster than a human should be able to move, she dove for the edge of the shack, while simultaneously throwing a countermeasure in the opposite direction.

Smart targeting is designed to direct subsequent fire to the first impact point, even on moving targets. But certain countermeasures can disrupt that feature. As a result, all of Jean's shots headed towards her thrown device instead, requiring him to change settings and relocate to a different firing position. He crawled out from under the tank but kept it between him and the shack. He knew she was injured, and realized that he needed to smoke her out before she had time to patch herself up and figure out an attack plan.

Jean lobbed a concussion grenade directly into the shack's doorway. Still *got it*, he thought with pride over the perfectly landed throw. The force of the explosion blew the roof off and further destroyed the entrance to make the building entirely inaccessible. He fired off a few more bursts for good measure and intently watched for movement.

Suddenly, a second explosion went off behind the shack. Due to its brightness and substantial amount of flames, Jean assumed it was the rocket pack. No one could survive *that*, he convinced himself. He lingered several minutes more, but detected nothing threatening.

He decided to inch his way around the tank to inspect his handiwork in defeating the third and final hunter of the three-round game. Jean cleared the corner of the tank at a snail's pace, but froze in his tracks when he noticed a glint of light from a grassy knoll a few dozen meters behind the ruined shack.

Jean didn't need to look down as searing hot pain enveloped his chest. He knew he'd been shot through the heart. He fell to his knees, and with his last ounce of strength, he managed a firm salute to his worthy foe. It was a gesture of respect from a former soldier to a Marine, before collapsing onto the soft desert foliage amongst the other dead military properties.

Sonya Kane, formerly a staff sergeant in the USMC and now a literal hired gun and Chief Hunter for the Rosen Games Network, approached her latest kill confidently but cautiously. She had left her rifle in the grass where it had just been used, but removed the sling to support her injured left shoulder. She came alongside Prisoner 24601, holstered the sidearm in her right hand, and returned the salute he had so honorably given to her.

Hunter Kane held that pose longer than she needed to. As she stood in the blood-speckled sand, she imagined the cheers likely erupting around the so-called civilized world for the close of one of the most challenging hunts she could recall.

Her victory gave her little comfort, though. Not only had she lost a couple more colleagues, she had also killed who she suspected was another fellow veteran... all for sport; a vet who seemed likely to have been specifically chosen to face off with *her* in the hunt. While she wasn't immune to pride, misgivings with the Network's recent contestants began to creep into her subconscious over the past several months, due in part to a few anonymous messages she had received. She knew something desperately needed to change about her lifestyle choices, and her future in general; she just didn't know how to go about making that happen.

Chapter One: Dereliction

Chicago – Government building, Dearborn Street

Milo Durron sat besieged at his desk while his office mates continued to rave about The Most Dangerous Game of the night before. He must've heard at least four times already how Kane set her rocket pack to explode so Jean would think her finished. He didn't know what surprised him more; that the brutal gladiatorial game was able to continue long after the Population Control Act was repealed, or that his fellow deputy US Marshals could be entertained by such a thing. Milo stood up in a huff, unable to tolerate any more deviant claptrap.

"Where you going Durron? You a Jean fan or something?" one of his colleagues asked mockingly.

"Just going down two floors to see if ATF has any contraband alcohol and tobacco I can swipe for lunch," Milo quipped as he exited the congested office corral.

Even at mid-morning a drink sounded good to him, so he headed toward the vending room for one of the non-alcoholic variety. Being a veteran of thirty years, he was far too traditional to drink on duty. Milo had no idea what he would buy when he got there, but when he heard his name yelled in angst down the hall he knew that decision no longer mattered.

"Durron!" Supervisor Jamey Kirlan breathed laboriously. "I'm glad I caught you Milo. We have a situation that may require your… unique expertise."

Kirlan becoming a supervisor was quite the mystery to everyone at the office for the first couple months of his transfer there. The way he got so sweaty and anxious in even the slightest of stressful situations made people wonder how he became a deputy marshal in the first place. Eventually, one of the office gossips found out that he had spent his entire career in the Financial Services Division. He was good with numbers, not so much with people it seemed.

Almost a year ago, Kirlan was given an ultimatum; choose another division to cross-train in or one would be chosen for him. Information Services and

Intelligence were filled up so he went with Prisoner Operations, or POD, and was given a temporary promotion in the Windy City to test his resolve. Despite supervisors not being needed in the field as much as regular deputies, promotion remained a difficult adaptation for him.

"Ok. What unique expertise are you referring to sir?" Milo asked, after letting the man catch his breath.

"There's been a prison break at Leavenworth" he answered, as he wiped his brow with one of his embroidered kerchiefs. "I understand you worked there for a time?"

"That's right. At the training center, for my last two years in the Army to finish off my thirty on active duty. How many got loose?"

"They're saying three... By 'they' I mean the task force that's waiting in the operations room for us. Waiting for *you* to be more specific."

Milo strode into the darkened operations room as casually as if he lived there, despite only having the occasional meeting in the windowless, government grey space. Supervisor Kirlan slunk in behind him and quietly took a seat in the corner. The task force's two men and one woman already seated, and an Army officer waited impatiently on the central monitor. His thick brow drooping lower as Milo sat.

"Well, now that we're all here..." the colonel began with disdain. "Our fugitives have had a head start of approximately twelve hours, give or take. The locals are coming up empty on leads for how the escape occurred, as well as any trails to where they may be headed."

The colonel inhaled to continue with his rant-like briefing, but one of the other men in the room cut him off.

"What have these men been charged with Colonel Takbrite? Can we get access to their service records? That may help in tracking them down and anticipating their next move."

A slight shimmer around the edges of the deputy who just spoke indicated that he wasn't really there. Milo sighed at having been fooled by another hologram projected into a chair. He subtly checked the table display dimly glowing in front of him, and discovered that he was the only real person in the room, aside from of course Kirlan, fighting to stave off an ulcer in the corner by the look of him.

Takbrite cleared his throat and continued. "You should have the service records before the end of this conversation, or most of them anyway. In regards to their charges, I'm afraid that's classified at the moment. We'll revisit that issue at a later date I'm sure. Anything else? Very well. As I was saying... representatives from your respective field offices were specifically selected not only of course due to proximity to the incident, but also because combined, your offices have the most experience in fugitive recovery of any other region in the continent."

The holograms from the Saint Louis, Lincoln, and Oklahoma City field offices glanced up at each other and shrugged. Milo sat up in his seat, finally realizing what seemed odd about the meeting of the virtual minds.

"Is this everyone working on the escape Colonel? Seems like an awfully small task force for such a high-profile situation."

The question seemed to annoy the oversized projection. "The usual bulletins will go out to the local PDs. As far as the size of the TF; if you were here a minute sooner, you would've learned that we're trying to keep as many noses out of this as we can by keeping a low profile. Also, this is only half the field agents because we're pairing experienced deputies with counterparts from the Army's Criminal Investigative Division," Takbrite answered without even looking up from whatever held his attention out of camera range.

Milo slouched back down, satisfied with the answer but still skeptical of the approach. He couldn't recall a single instance where Army CID not only worked on a fugitive case like this directly, but also aligned with an outside agency on equal jurisdictional footing to their own.

"Now then," Takbrite continued, "with pleasantries finally out of the way, you'll notice mission briefings appear on your secure in-boxes, code-named Rubicon. You're all getting the same information so there's little-to-no redundancy. Let's go get em."

The colonel's image abruptly vanished precisely when the chime of a new message arrived. The digital deputies nodded at each other and faded like the ghosts they were. The lights automatically returned to their normal intensity of a sleepy-dim, faux twilight level. Looking around the room, Milo always liked to admire the paintings of old Chicago, alternating with pictures of early Marshals and other federal agents. He looked down to regard his unopened case file and sighed.

"Good pep talk coach," Milo retorted to what he thought was an empty room. He then jerked his head over to see Kirlan snoozing in the corner, and grinned to himself at the irony the lack of excitement the case seemed to be inspiring.

Chapter Two: Old Friends

The trip from Chicago to north east Kansas didn't take anywhere near as long as it used to, thanks to flying cars and the open sky lanes of the lesser-populated Midwest. It was made particularly short with the speed and classic comfort of his new Studebaker Sky Hawk II thought Milo. He could never afford such a luxurious vehicle on even double his pay, but the car was donated to a regional contest for the American Legion, and he had won. The only time in his life he had ever won anything of note.

Studebaker had shocked the world when it went back in business a hundred years to the day its main plant in South Bend, Indiana had closed its doors in 1963. A pair of the original owners' great-grandchildren had gambled on reinventing the company from a name lost to history, and the risks paid off. In an era where most car companies had either gone under or been absorbed by others, offering a stylish, sleek choice alternative to the universally boxy look created by the remaining auto designers, had been an instant boon for the former failed company.

The ride was so smooth that Milo almost forgot to finish reading his portion of the mission documents. It seems things were quite straight-forward, which was no surprise to him considering the lack of details during the briefing. Due to his familiarity with the oldest military installation west of the Mississippi River, he was directed to look for any discrepancies at *both* Kansas facilities, Departments of Defense and Corrections, as well as its personnel who had contact with the fugitives.

Milo briefly circled the non-restricted airspace above the Fort before landing in the visitor's lot. He had to check his readouts to make sure he'd actually landed, because the touchdown was so soft he wasn't sure it had even happened. He stepped out into the warm, Midwest morning sun and shielded his eyes to take in the all-too-familiar view. He closed the scissor-door of his Studebaker and turned to look up at the imposing towers of the US Army Disciplinary Barracks of Fort Leavenworth. Most of the original facility, with its last major renovation completed in 2002, still remained, but multiple additions and updates had been made in the interim.

Milo's final active-duty posting was actually as an instructor of 'command doctrine' for the Army's Combined Arms Center, which was a stone's throw away from the prison grounds. However, he frequently visited the military's only maximum security prison to provide examples of what poor leadership and discipline could cause. With some spectacular exceptions, many of the inmates held within the stone and steel walls of the prison were there due to a breakdown of consistency and command structure, in Milo's purview anyway. The old saying of 'idle hands are the devil's playground' always came to mind when he took his students to the prison.

The briefing from Colonel Takbrite claimed Milo's Criminal Investigation Division counterpart would meet him there, but the place was eerily quiet. There were only three other vehicles in the lot, and not another person could be seen in his quick scan of the area. Milo began walking toward the visitor's entrance when a familiar face, wearing *pristine* a class-A uniform, came striding his way. The man stopped about five meters from him and presented a picture-perfect salute.

"Good morning Master Sergeant Durron. Welcome back to Leavenworth sir."

"At ease Carter, there's no master here," Milo conceded. "I see they made you a three-stripe. Who did you con to make that happen?"

Sargent Jacen Carter grinned, but that was the only part of him that moved. "Didn't have to con anyone sir. I just told my captain you taught me everything you know over a week or two, and he shrugged and went back to ogling Sonya Kane."

Milo nodded and ignored the jab at his six-month course. "Seems about right. What's this I hear about a jail break from your house? This isn't the Tibetan front where you can let people come and go you know."

Carter could let a lot of things slide, but not when his integrity came into question. The dire look he gave Milo sent a chill from head to toe.

"The escape occurred when the three prisoners were being transferred from here to Big Top. It was on BOPs watch, not mine, sir. The transfer itself looked fishy to me, but those decisions are above my paygrade."

Although just down the road, the civilian-run United States Penitentiary wasn't under military jurisdiction. The Bureau of Prisons controlled that installation, as well as a few others in the area, though not *nearly* to the same standards.

"Fishy how Carter? And please, you can drop the 'sir' rigamarole."

"I give respect where it is due, sir," Carter admitted with a sheepish grin. "For starters, the transfer was fishy because, as far as I could tell, Watson, Powell, and Hyde should never have been sent here in the first place. None of their charges appeared to be military related, nor did maximum security seem warranted in any of their cases, sir."

Milo cradled his chin in his hand, similar in a way to The Thinker statue in Paris; a habit that had been the source of relentless criticism throughout his adult life. He noticed Carter staring and smirking so he adjusted his posture.

"So... you know their charges? Are you able to provide them to me? Takbrite said they were classified, which didn't sit well with me."

"Classified? To a Marshal? That sir is surprising. Watson became a government contractor after his time with the SEALS. He went off the radar on mission in Eastern Europe somewhere for a few days; when he resurfaced he was charged with breach of contract and selling military secrets.

"Powell was on terminal leave and got picked up for DUI. Hyde had just been given an other-than-honorable discharge for statutory rape of an officer's daughter. Those would fall under Articles 106, 111, and 120 respectively sir, but none were filed through the Uniform Code of Military Justice. I checked their paperwork myself, sir."

"Thorough as usual Carter," Milo mused as his hand briefly drifted back to his chin. Jacen was right; none of those cases should've automatically been sent to prison, particularly Leavenworth's unique take on maximum-security detention.

"Carter, I've reviewed their service records, but they'd been severely redacted. Is there some connection between these three men that isn't immediately apparent on file? Their collaboration seems awfully convenient to me."

"Couldn't say sir, other than maybe their advanced training. They all served on one special team or another. At least that's what the other investigator pointed out, but I don't think he intended for me to hear that."

"Yes, perhaps that's the common denominator... Wait. What other investigator?" Milo asked, looking up at Carter for the first time in a few moments.

"The CID investigator. I believe he said his name was Karrde, spelled with a K and double R he deliberately pointed out. He was supposed to meet you here but arrived just before you did. Apologies for not mentioning it sooner sir."

"Damn! How'd he get here so fast? Guess I'm not the only one not keen on this arrangement. Where's he gotten off to?"

"I don't have an answer to your first question sir, but he apparently already knew a lot of the intel you didn't. He's likely talking to BOP about their version of events as we speak, just up the way there as you're well aware."

Milo slumped in his stance somewhat. The revelation of being two steps behind in less than two hours of getting assigned to a case was *not* what he would call starting out on the right foot. The case file claimed Karrde was tasked out of a base in Nevada. The only way he could've arrived before him is if Karrde knew about the escape long before he did. Equal partnership indeed, he scoffed.

"Copy that. I guess there's some catching up to be done here, so I'd better get to it. Good to see you again Jacen. Keep up the good fight Sarge."

"Will do sir. Let me know if I can be of any more assistance." Carter snapped to attention and gave one more salute before spinning on his heel and heading back inside."

Chapter Three: New Enemies

Milo jumped into his Stude and raced the six kilometers to the BOP office down the road. He made it to their landing pad in a few minutes, but it was plenty of time for his suspicions to grow. The case couldn't be further from proper procedure, by his reckoning at least. He also began to wonder how the other teams between the Marshals and CID were faring. Although he didn't know the other deputies, he had worked with people from their respective field offices, and intended to check in with them about their thoughts on his current situation, if time permitted.

Then there was the CID half of the task force. Though officially titled Criminal Investigation Command, most still referred to the investigative wing of the Army's active duty and civilian-run organization as the CID. Army special agents were upstanding investigators, for all things Army related, but they didn't typically follow cases in the traditional sense. Those duties were often left to other agencies, or at least they used to be.

As he exited the car, his mind wondered where this Agent Karrde thought he was going alone and out of his element. He approached the BOP penitentiary, known as Big Top, but the imposing, domed structure of its namesake had long been replaced by a less majestic building of the standard featureless modern design. A man with obvious military bearing, but trying very hard to hide it, was rushing out the darkened glass doors of the visitor's entrance. He was wearing a utilitarian light blue mock turtleneck sweater with grey business slacks, which had nearly hidden pockets along the sides. His tan, half-trench mackintosh swayed behind him like a cape, and he was long past caring what his hazel hair looked like.

"Where's the fire pal?" Milo asked, deliberately standing in the other's way. The man was so focused on his flex tablet that they nearly collided.

"Ah! What? Do you mind? I have some fugitives to track down before one of you ne'er-do-wells lose them or get them killed."

There's a term you don't hear every day, Milo mused. "Huh, small world, I'm here for the exact same reason. Deputy Marshal Durron. I just came from USDB to find an Agent Karrde from Army CID. Can you point me in his, or her, direction?"

The slightly shorter man, with light blue eyes to almost perfectly match his sweater, gave Milo a confused look, then one of abashed suspicion. "That would be me; though I'm not going to point at myself. Will Karrde. I gather that means you're with me Milton. So let's get move... What's that look for?"

"First, the name's Milo, not Milton. Second, the look was just me thinking about all the names you were probably called growing up."

Karrde gave Milo a stern glare. "What makes you think I grew up?"

Yeah, I can work with this guy, Milo thought. "So where we off to chief?"

Another strange glance from Will. "I'll fill you in once we're in the air. Hop in, we'll take my... Wait. Is that your Sky Hawk over there?"

Milo peered over at the dark blue government issued vehicle and grinned. "Why yes it is. I won it in a contest put on by the Legion."

"Of course you did," Karrde responded in the same suspicious manner many people did about the Studebaker. "No matter; you drive."

~

The gleaming, silver mist-colored Studebaker lifted off and jetted due west, away from the sun in the cloudless morning sky. A motionless figure, seated in a black Citroën Aircross, watched the sleek vehicle until it had disappeared into the hazy blue from the southern edge of the prison's visitor parking lot. The shadow of a person knew where they were going, and why, but didn't want to spook them by suspecting a tail too soon. When a plan such as this is set in motion, most people in a similar position would simply sit back and watch, manipulating probabilities every so often to further their amusement. But this wasn't one of those plans. Eventually, direct interference would have to be undertaken, forcing events to become treacherously unpredictable. That moment was a long way off however; at least that was the current forecast. The timetable depended entirely on those two federal agents, who were likely halfway to their next clue. It was time to go. Not after the two men, but several steps ahead of them. If they were any good at their jobs, they

wouldn't need another clue until the next logical step --
a face-to-face encounter.

~

The forty-minute trek west had been a mostly
unproductive one. Once Milo was able to get anything
out of Karrde, unrelated to his car that is, he learned the
BOP transport vehicle their escapees were in was located
just outside of Colorado Springs. There was still time in
the journey to put a few pieces together, before his
passenger clammed up again. Milo just had to prod a
little more forcefully until he struck a nerve.

"Do any of our fugitives have a connection to
Peterson Air Force Base, or Cheyenne Mountain?" Milo
asked in an attempt to keep Karrde focused.

Special Agent Will Karrde was back to burying his
face into his flex tablet. "If memory serves, Hyde was
with Space Command before his other-than-honorable
discharge. I believe he was on the Colonial Response
Force during the Mars colony riot. I'm not sure about
that though. What does his service record say?"

"Couldn't tell you," Milo answered with some
frustration seeping through. "I only skimmed the records
I received, but they were so redacted and edited by
Takbrite's people he might as well have not sent them at

all. Why do I get the feeling I'm being sand-bagged here?"

Will jerked his head to regard Milo. He stared at him intently for several seconds before answering. "Probably because you *are*, Deputy Durron. I've been blocked requesting records through DOD at every turn that might prove helpful, and there's little doubt Takbrite is personally responsible for that obstruction. Also, and I'm sure it comes as no surprise, BOP is being completely uncooperative. All my info comes from a series of strings I had to pull to even get started."

Milo sighed, realizing he's more in the dark than he thought. "That's all well and good, but where does that leave *us*? Are you out of strings, and do I get a buy-in on any of them, now that we're working together on this?"

"I suppose that leaves us exactly where we are right now; following our only lead that will hopefully point us toward the next one," Will countered defensively as he turned toward the window. "That said, I'm afraid my sources are confidential... for now. I'm just as uncomfortable about this arrangement as you are Deputy Durron. We'll just have to trust each other."

Milo canted his head contemptuously to respond, but kept his pessimistic comments to himself, on the one rare occasion he was able to do so. Karrde couldn't possibly expect him to trust the man in the thirty minutes they'd known each other. Professional courtesy was one thing, trust was something else entirely.

They approached the coordinates of the misappropriated prison vehicle. It was remarkably well hidden, considering it had practically crashed on its right side only a few meters from a public highway in light brush. Milo passed over the boxy, unmarked transport van before deciding on a spot to land. As the engine shut down, he turned to give Will an askance look.

"Right," Karrde said scanning the area. "Where the hell is everybody?" The wooded hollow, where the transport made what appeared to be an uncontrolled landing, was completely deserted. Just two intrepid investigators regarding a partially camouflaged government van next to a quiet asphalt thoroughfare was all that occupied the serene space. In another context, Milo considered, the place could easily become a romantic tryst site.

"Where did the intel about this vehicle's location come from again?" Milo asked with suspicion, and a touch of sarcasm.

Will scoffed but didn't look toward Milo when he answered. "NORAD cued me in actually. They reported a low flying, fast-moving vehicle headed west trying to stay below radar. Those guys... they *had* to know that modern radar and listening networks can spot a literal fly on the wall."

"Not quite what I'm asking Karrde," Milo accused. The North American Aerospace Defense Command has been guarding the skies over the US and Canada since the mid-1960s. They see practically everything airborne on the continent, but they also don't keep many people on speed-dial either.

"Your cryptic sarcasm is no match for my jaded witticisms," Will replied with a smirk. "Besides, we're practically in NORAD's backyard. You can even see Cheyenne from here. Not a stretch of the imagination to assume this was our wayward transport."

He had a point, Milo conceded. But that still didn't explain how Karrde got that report so quickly. "I'll call a tech team out here. No offense, but I have more faith in our people's equipment and experience than CID's. Besides, I don't think this sort of evidence collection and processing is your ilk's forte anyway."

"None taken. I was going to suggest that very thing actually. In the meantime we'll have to figure out who gave them a ride from here. The transport appears to still be functional, for the most part. This hollow might've been just a rendezvous point; a somewhat popular one by the looks of it. They could be to Denver by now."

"Well, you said Hyde's last duty station was here right?" Milo deduced, as his hand came back up to his chin. "And his arrest and subsequent discharge was brought on by statutory rape allegations from a General... If I were a betting man, I'd wager that young lady will know at least *something* about this situation."

Will nodded his head in amusement. "I'll take that bet, unless there's some nonsensical hook attached to it."

"What's the problem Karrde, afraid you might teach me something in the process?" Milo asked challengingly, crossing his arms.

"Very well. How about... the terms are for currency to suit the culture we live in; data. Loser reveals a source of the victor's choice."

"What could I *possibly* know that you don't at this point?"

"For starters, the details of Hyde's arrest. It's not on any of the reports I've read. In fact, I didn't know it was *statutory* rape. Just assumed it was the regular variety.

"In that case, deal," Milo confidently responded as he extended his hand. Will promptly grasped it and shook firmly. "It'd probably be safer *for me* to bet with actual money, but prepare to have some names ready Karrde. She can't be far. Generals tend to live close to their posts."

Chapter Four: Betrothed

Jaina Isard, seventeen-year-old daughter of General Joben Isard, resided at the family estate in Manitou Springs, according to Air Force records. The Isard family created quite the dynasty within the AF, particularly in the multiple bases of the region.

After graduating from the Air Force Academy just north of Colorado Springs, Joben was able to pick wherever he wanted to serve. To the surprise of everyone who knew him, Joben decided to take a captain position at NORAD; a post with little advancement opportunity. Not a year later, he surprised everyone again when he announced the creation of Space Command's elite Colonial Response Force. The CRF was promptly put in charge of securing the many fledgling colonies in the solar system and beyond, to protect and defend against situations like the riots that had befallen one of the lunar stations.

Making rank came very easy for him after that. Once he became a senior colonel, well on his way to a one-star general, he had bid for and was granted the prestigious position of Commandant of the Academy. The man chose to make the military his life, so he shocked the military world a third time when articles began to arise about him not only taking the time to meet a woman from an affluent family and marry her, but also having three, high-achieving children in what seemed like too short a time to accomplish those admirable feats. The least surprising part of his story however, was that General Isard was *very* protective of his youngest child and only daughter, Jaina. Reading between the lines of the file attached to Milo's task force documents, the General's response when he discovered who his daughter was dating seemed akin to calling in Special Forces to retrieve a lost dog.

The two investigators were setting down in the front courtyard of the spacious Isard estate when Will realized he had no plan, which could quickly reach uncomfortable levels given the high profile of the family whose door they were primed to knock on. Milo noticed the look of near panic on his partner's face. "Don't worry, I'll do the talking. I actually have a teenage daughter, so hopefully they'll have something in com... mon."

His train of thought was interrupted by a very tall, auburn-haired girl running out the front door in tears. Will rolled up his flex tablet at the sound and the two men exchanged puzzled glances. They exited the car in haste, not knowing the reason she was fleeing from her stately home in such a distressed manner.

"They took it!" The girl cried in a sob. "They stole my car and threatened to kill me if I told anyone they were here!"

"Calm down ma'am," Milo soothed. "You're safe now. We're with the police. Now, who took your car?"

She sniffed a couple times before answering. "The guys who just escaped from prison. Aren't you here about that?" Her question was a bit lighter on the whimpers, Milo noticed.

"About escaped prisoners? What would they be doing here?"

"I... I don't know. I went to meet my boyfriend and they were there." The crying had almost ceased by that point, and her tone took on a defensive turn.

"You mean the 22-year-old boyfriend whom your father had arrested, and who just broke out of Leavenworth with two others?" Will finally cut in, not being able to keep silent any longer.

Milo slowly turned to regard the man. He gave Will a subtly stern look with raised eyebrows, indicating for him to stop talking. Milo turned back to whom he confidently knew was Jaina Isard, giving her a similar, yet softer, glare. She stood agape with her eyes darting frantically between the two men.

"How long ago did they leave, Miss Isard?" Milo continued in even tones.

"Uh, about thirty minutes ago, I think."

"And how many were in your car when it was taken?"

"Two... I mean three," she corrected desperately.

Both men looked at each other knowingly, and then sprinted for the front door. Milo drew his sidearm while Will talked on his embedded mobile. Jaina stood screaming threats of calling her father if they went into the house. When they reached the door however, her threats turned to pleas, fearing for her culpability of the situation and the safety of the fugitive she was harboring.

On instinct, once Milo burst through the doorway, he immediately ran up the massive staircase, not phased in the least by the immaculate oak paneling and intricate crown molding. Will had the opposite reaction. He stood in awe of the eighteenth century, Scandinavian architecture, with scores of military memorabilia tastefully on display throughout the foyer. The entryway looked like it had come straight out of the Gilded Age of nineteenth century American architecture. An age, Will recalled, that was one of the more short-lived, for several good reasons.

Milo's swift, yet methodical footfalls on the second floor snapped Will out of his veneration. He quickly scanned the large, but empty, first floor rooms. Dining room, kitchen, den; all beautifully rendered, but seemingly unlived in. They were kept in pristine condition, with neither dust nor clutter; but even with an army of clean staff it was obvious the rooms were rarely used. Almost like they were guest showrooms, or rented spaces for events.

Loud scuffling on the second level compelled Will to finally pull out his weapon. He reached the lodge-like foyer when he spotted a very lean young man descending the wraparound staircase two steps at a time, recognizing him immediately.

"Hold it Hyde! It already looks bad enough for you Marcus. Don't make me add assault of a federal officer on top of everything else."

The naturally tan form that was Marcus Hyde slowly put his hands up, while also clearing the remaining steps. "Charge me with whatever you please sir," Hyde responded coolly in a thick Cajun accent. "Nothing I done so far would give reason to send me to maximum security. I just assume you shoot me rather than send me back where I didn't belong in the first place."

Will slightly lowered his aim but remained on target. "I agree with you Marcus. Come with me, now, before the cavalry gets here, and I promise to do what I can so you don't go back there. I'm here to help, you see?"

Hyde took a step toward Will, prompting him to raise his gun back up. "I *am* the cavalry mister," said Hyde, "Second Colonial Cavalry out of Mars station

Acheron. And I don't believe you. Not after what's happened to me."

"I know that Marcus. I also know *why* this is happening to you. How you got out with Watson and Parker, and..."

"That wasn't my fault!" Hyde boomed. "The other two said they didn't know what was going on either, but the prison transport malfunctioned and Parker was somehow able to take control. So I said to come he..."

Hyde suddenly went rigid then collapsed on the floor. Will spotted the stun bolt between his shoulder blades and looked up to see Milo cautiously making his way down the large staircase with gun in hand.

"You let him get too close. One lunge and he would've had you. I've seen what these space soldiers can do and, some offense, but I don't think you could've handled him. Not the way I've seen you move."

Will smirked and holstered his sidearm. "Good thing I let you tag along then," he jested attempting to get even for the 'some offense' comment. "I set up a recall on my car to pick me up when we found the prison transport. It should have tracked me here by now, I suspect."

"Tired of my driving already?" Milo cuffed a groggy Hyde, and each man took an arm to lead him outside. "Is this where the jurisdictional pissing contest begins?"

"Not for me it doesn't. I just thought my car would be more appropriate, since it has restraints in the back. Besides, I wouldn't want anything to happen to your Stude..."

Will trailed off when he noticed the small throng that awaited them outside in the courtyard. Most wore maroon and grey jumpsuits with an unfamiliar logo emblazoned on it. The remaining men and women, however, had the telltale look of Bureau of Prisons employees; not to mention the bold yellow BOP on their navy blue jackets.

"Deputy Durron. Agent Karrde. We have an affidavit for the custody of this man, signed by the governor. As a fellow Justice Department employee Mister Durron, we thank you for the safe recovery of this fugitive."

Will was immediately on the defensive. "We haven't even been here twenty minutes! How did you get the governor's signature on something he couldn't possibly know about already?"

The stuffy, unkempt BOP man diverted his sleepy gaze from Milo to Will in a robotic manner. "The times we live in Agent Karrde. We all have our orders, do we not? You've done your part, now it's our turn to do ours."

"Who did you call when we got here?" Milo whispered out of the corner of his mouth.

"Don't let them take me," Hyde pleaded. "You gave me your word."

The men in jumpsuits moved to encircle the BOP representative in the cheap suit, who stood at the foot of the expertly designed stone steps beneath Milo, Will, and Hyde. Will opened his mouth to further protest, but thought better of it. His shoulders slumped in a defeated manner, which was felt by the other two in sequence.

"I'm sorry Marcus, but it doesn't look like today is our day." His eyes turned to the increasingly smug BOP man. "I expect this man to be treated with the respect he is due, mister... I'm sorry, I didn't catch your name."

"No, I don't believe you did, Agent Karrde," the Prisons man said with a smirk. "He will be given the highest of honors we can offer, I assure you."

With that, four of the people in jumpsuits ascended the stairs to take custody of Hyde. They courteously swapped out Milo's cuffs for theirs and returned them to the deputy. The fugitive was utterly speechless, and Milo caught a glimpse of terror in the young man's eyes as he was led away. He exploded out of his listlessness as he was being stuffed into their transport van, one that was nearly identical to the absconded one from earlier, but the desperate act was quickly quelled by a stun gun.

In a few short moments, the congested courtyard was just as clear as when they had arrived, aside from Will's dingy blue government vehicle nearby. The high stone walls, with small ramparts lining the top as if it were small-scale castle walls, overshadowed the now desolate area that gave Will a trapped feeling he hadn't experienced earlier. Much like the ground level of the house, the courtyard gave off a sense of abandonment.

"So about our bet," Milo began as they watched the other transports drift over the western horizon. "I think I'm gonna need more than just one question answered. I'll make a list for you, so I don't forget anything."

Chapter Five: Looking Glass

The standoff with Bureau of Prisons, and the unknown jumpsuited entity, had ended as quickly as it began. Before the pair made their way back to their respective cars, they remembered there was one more person who witnessed the events they had to finish interviewing. They tracked down a crestfallen Jaina cowering inside a gazebo at the north end of the courtyard.

They promised not to tell her father what had happened, in exchange for any information on her stolen vehicle, and the direction the remaining two escapees may have been headed. Once the threat of instant discovery passed, she became quite helpful by detailing how her father tracked the vehicle. Although she said she didn't see the car leave, she claimed that 'the smart one' said they were going south. To Milo and

Will however, that meant they were actually planning to travel north.

For the second time, Milo was surprised that Will had acquiesced to following US Marshal protocol, and not CID's, by not reporting to the nearest Army field office. They were back in the air and speeding toward Denver. Will had sent his car ahead to the nearest Criminal Investigation Division office to give the impression they had separated; yet another questionable tactic. After a few silent minutes, it was Milo's turn to receive a new message chime. His dashboard display indicated that it was the preliminary report for the prison transport. Will didn't appear interested in what the Marshal's forensic team found, but Milo read it over thoroughly, after setting his car on autopilot.

"I don't want to alarm you," Milo warned sarcastically, "but there may have been foul play involved in the commandeering of that transport."

"You don't say," Will responded with equal disdain. "Let me guess, a device was discovered on an external programming port that allowed the inmates access to the control-settings. And that device has no distinguishing marks on it to trace."

Milo switched back to manual piloting and decelerated to nearly a complete stop. "All right, spill it Karrde. What did you mean when you told Hyde you knew why he was sent to Leavenworth? Who are you chatting with on that tablet of yours?"

Will rolled up his flex tablet and sighed. "Was I right about the transport or not?"

"They found evidence there *was* a device where you said, yes, but it had burned itself up to the point where the team could not extract any data. That's close enough for me to know that we're not on the same page."

Another sigh. "I don't have definitive proof yet, but I have reason to believe the Bureau of Prisons has a back-door partnership with the Rosen Network to procure highly skilled inmates to perform in some of their... morally questionable programs. And have been recruiting for them over the past few years at least, for a nominal fee I presume."

All Milo could do was stare at the man. His mind tried to analyze a dozen lines of inquiry to make sense out of what Will had just revealed. He had to admit, there was a certain amount of logic to the claim. But such a lucrative arrangement would leave too many loose ends for an agency that kept secrets like a sieve held water.

"To what end? BOP hasn't changed their ways in a hundred years. How could they make a deal of this magnitude without anyone finding out?"

"This is where it gets murky. I couldn't say how they're keeping this *one* thing under wraps, but the most obvious way would be to keep this knowledge extremely limited. This elusive agreement also allows them to keep their prisoner numbers up, but the correctional officers impressively low."

"Funding would remain maxed out," Milo mulled out loud, "but that doesn't explain what keyed you onto it. How long have your people suspected this?"

Will's tablet chimed but he resisted looking at the message he had received, barely. "I can only tell you that I've been working on this for about two years. Everything else is before my time on the assignment. Can we move along now?" he asked, as he finally gave in to check what had been so incessantly for vying for his attention.

"I'm not sure which way we should be going," Milo answered exasperatedly. "Heading to Denver was just a guess on my part, but your intel seems to be much better than mine. So, mister super spy, where should we be racing to?"

Will's head snapped over to regard Milo intently for a long moment; he then went back to a message of particular significance. "As luck would have it, we have a lead on Jaina Isard's car. Seems as though she really *did* know all her father's tricks to track her whereabouts. No surprise there I suppose."

When Will didn't elaborate after several seconds, Milo sat back in a huff. This guy must be new to the whole partnership scene, he thought. Keeping secrets as a way to boost a feeling of self-worth was one thing, but not leaving enough scraps to make educated decisions and satisfy suspicion was a clear sign of amateurism.

"Sorry," Will finally responded. "I just wanted to be sure. The Isard's Aerocar had a regular tracking device, which was disabled almost immediately. But there are two others that ping on different frequencies at random intervals when in motion. The last ping gave a location in Boulder…"

Milo didn't wait for him to finish before he hit the accelerator. They were off as if the Sky Hawk had a hyperdrive. He adjusted their heading slightly to the west of their original destination of Denver. The heads-up display indicated the trip would be 26 minutes at their current speed and heading; plenty of time to work on the basic trust issues that continued to plague their forced alliance.

~

Since Will's government vehicle was nearly to Denver by the time they were en route to Boulder, he re-directed it to their new target for a brief surveillance of the area. The National brand vehicle was a no-frills model when it came to comfort or performance, but its scanning equipment came close to rivaling a modern reconnaissance drone. In fact, the surveillance package was likely worth more than the car itself.

"Looks like they torched it," Will volunteered from the scan results of Jaina's stolen car and surrounding vicinity. "Whatever her cover story to her father was, it may need some revision. The car was left in an abandoned lot not far from the regional airport. That's a little on the nose, don't you think?"

"And here I thought I'd be the only one to find that odd," Milo chimed in. Will turned his way with a puzzled look on his face.

"Consider who we're chasing here. Watson is a highly skilled and decorated intelligence agent, and Parker was with Marine Recon. Both are trained to blend in and not draw attention to themselves. Where does setting a stolen car on fire near a transportation hub play into that?"

Will regarded him for another long moment before answering. His steel blue eyes danced in thought. Eventually, he slumped in concession with his head digging into the soft leather seat.

"I was being facetious earlier, but you evidently think it's a ruse. Security would likely be too tight at airports to risk using anyway... at least for both of them together."

"Well, I hadn't considered them splitting up, but they would've quickly realized their chances of getting caught go up the longer they're together. So yeah, they're definitely trying to throw us off. What do you suppose their plan from here might be?"

Will turned back to his flex tablet and vigorously manipulated its interface. The pair had passed Denver, and Milo could see the Boulder skyline quickly approaching. Milo didn't want to rush Will, but it would waste precious seconds to make a detour once they'd passed any potential leads. It served no purpose to check the burned sports car. Milo recalled the forensic team from earlier and redirected them to Boulder as a potential answer came to Will.

"There's a high-speed train station just beyond the airport from the direction of where the car was burned. A hover train just departed westbound." Will turned and smiled at Milo. "Do you think this thing can catch it?"

Milo's response was a grin as he pressed the accelerator as far as it would go. The Stude swerved to the left, and the magno-rails hover trains used to defy gravity became visible in seconds. While interstate hover trains were relatively safe and reliable, the downside to pursuing one was that they didn't actually make full stops, except at major transit ports. There were designated transfer points at various locations where entire passenger carriages were smoothly removed at one point, and others, either empty, or partially occupied, were latched onto the train a few seconds later.

Finding a vehicle that could keep up with its near-supersonic speed was hard to come by, unless one had access to military craft. The new Studebakers were supposed to be faster than the average domestic cars, but certainly not Mach one to overtake it at full speed. Milo just hoped the next station was near enough for the train to slow so they could catch up with their quarry.

"These things move faster than I remember," Milo begrudgingly conceded. The rails a purple blur from their ultraviolet light beneath them. "What's the next major stop?"

"Salt Lake City it looks like," Will read from his three millimeter thick flexible sheet for a tablet. "But carriages fourteen through ten disengage at various stations along the way. The next mid-sized transfer point is only a few minutes out. The train will have to slow down to swap out the carriages. I'll alert local police at those stations about our wayward friends."

"Good," Milo added. "That'll give me time to land on their ops car. I was afraid you might have to jump," he finished with a sly tenting of his brow.

"Aren't those operations spaces reserved for engineers and Transportation Marshalls?"

"Probably, but the average engineer doesn't know the difference between Homeland Security Marshalls and US Marshals anyway. I'm betting that whoever might challenge us is either ignorant of that, or apathetic to the whole situation.

Will nodded in agreement. "No bet from me. That's a much more doable plan than me jumping anyway… not as daring and heroic though."

"Feel free to jump out the door any time pal. All right, there it is. I think we might just make it! Hold on, this'll likely be an uncomfortable landing."

Chapter Six: On a Rail

The wave of nausea Will endured after the high-speed landing had subsided shortly after Milo showed his credentials to the middle-aged Latino man working alone in the operations car. Oscar, the hover train's lone engineer and likely only employee, barely looked up when the two men entered the room; an occurrence they both doubted was common enough to merit such a flippant response.

The small, dim space was completely covered with displays, gauges, and jumping readings of countless goings on throughout the train. Milo doubted they could all be effectively monitored by just one person. However, the most difficult part of the job, he deduced, was either to elude vertigo, or stay awake for a whole shift. It was obvious which of those two the technician struggled with.

They had reached the door to the first in a string of passenger carriages when Will remembered one important detail. "Is there open access to all compartments within the entire train?"

Oscar slowly spun in his chair to face them, and had a look of both contemplation and fatigue, as though this was the most work he had done all shift. "Everywhere except the long-distance sleeper car; number seven. When you get there use the call box and I can let you in. It'll be the display panel on your left." He then robotically turned back to the hypnotic readouts scrolling across his multiple screens.

Will and Milo nodded simultaneously and departed the car. Will checked to see if his sidearm was still on stun, and Milo took out his rapid imbedded identification device, or RIID. The device pings all personal ID chips within a seven meter radius. Any chips that don't match the person they're physically looking at, or ones that don't register on the scanner for various reasons, will be immediately recognized. Will hoped it would make the search of the train much easier, but Milo was worried the train might be full of people with active warrants.

The first three carriages were relatively straightforward passengers: commuters, vacationers, and people transiting who couldn't afford to fly. As soon as the pair entered the fourth carriage however, they knew something was off. The most obvious difference, they noted, was that the lighting was significantly dimmer. The dusk-like environment had a circadian effect on the passengers; most of them were either asleep, or close to it. The mid-October weather was also fortuitous for the passengers in the carriage. Well over half of them were using their jackets as blankets. Thankfully, sleeping or not, most of their faces were still visible for the RIID to make a positive ID. However, any who were covered or facing the window had to be roused.

They were about to pass into the next carriage when Milo stopped at the last row. He nudged Will with his elbow to get his attention, but once he took a couple steps back Will knew to take out his selective variable repeater, model six; standard government issue sidearm.

Facing the window, with a beat-up raincoat covering a person's entire body down to the shoes, sat someone who almost melted into the corner seat. The stained, brown coat nearly perfectly matched the brown and grey color scheme of the carriage's wall carpeting, particularly in the dim light. The dramatic difference in that carriage was starting to make sense.

Milo showed Will the reading from his RIID, which displayed an 'Unreadable PIC' message. This indicated the man had a chip that couldn't be read by even a government device, and prompted the two to share knowing glances. There were only a few logical reasons to receive that message. Damaged and altered ID chips were the most common in Milo's experience, but certain types of military and federal chips required a very specific reader in order to even be pinged.

Will opened his mouth to ask the dozing passenger to lower the coat, when the train unexpectedly jerked forward to slow down for the next transfer station. The man hiding in the corner took advantage of the distraction. In an explosion of fabric he burst out of his seat, slammed into Will, and threw the dingy raincoat onto him, making a break for the next carriage.

It all seemed to happen simultaneously and left Milo wondering if he should give chase or help Will off the poor woman who just received a rude awakening from him toppling onto her. Milo grabbed Will with one hand and heaved him to his feet. He left the coat covering Will's head and pulled out his own SVR-6 with his left hand, not breaking his stride in pursuit. Though he saw the large, cunning man exit the aft door of carriage five, Milo retrieved his RIID just in case he tried another disappearing trick. He felt the vibration of someone running up behind him but didn't turn around.

"Did we lose him? Is he in here?" Will asked in somewhat of a restrained calm.

"Pretty sure he's not in this carriage, but I'm not taking any chances. Get on that call box and have Oscar lock down the sleeper car right away."

Milo could tell Will didn't like being ordered around by him, but he was too focused on scanning the area to care at that particular moment. Nervous stares from passengers who noticed two men with guns drawn were starting to accumulate. Milo, however, was watching for the person who knew they were there but didn't react the same way most others were.

Will was on the line with Oscar as Milo entered the vestibule between carriages five and six. Milo reached for the controls to open the door to number six when his RIID reported another unreadable PIC. This meant one of two things: the guy was camping out in the lavatory, which he didn't consider feasible given the man's tactics thus far, or he had somehow hidden himself in the vestibule.

Milo tried to contain his mounting apprehension as the door in front of him smoothly slid aside. He tensed instinctively when the door behind him opened a second afterwards. He relaxed some when he recognized the huff from Will, but he didn't want to signal that they may be in imminent danger.

"All secure back there? That fall didn't look too healthy, you ok?"

Will looked at him like they were meeting for the first time, and the impression was less than positive. "Yes and yes," he answered with impatience. "Why do you care about my welfare all of a sudden?"

Milo's eyes slowly tilted upward, and Will cued into what he was indicating quickly but subtly. They both backed into their respective doorways when a dark figure dropped from the archway of the vestibule, knocking them both down in the process. The man was clearly an expert martial artist; fast and precise in his attacks, but not excessively violent or arrogant by following up with taunts.

For the second time in five minutes, Will was off his feet. The level of humiliation and frustration was reaching a point he hadn't felt since the war. He didn't recover nearly as fast as he did then, but at least this time he had a target to shoot at. Will fired two stun bolts at the man who was already over halfway through carriage six. The guy's body seized up and he stumbled a bit, but steadied himself on one of the seat backs. As he did so, Will got a clear look at his face to confirm he was Darius Parker.

After a few seconds to regain his balance, Parker continued to the aft door. Milo had risen to one knee and fired two more stun bolts into Parker's back. They clearly hit their mark, but had even less effect than the bolts fired by Will's weapon.

Parker reached the door laboriously, while the pair ran down the passageway identifying themselves as police and yelling for people to stay in their seats. Milo felt a twinge of relief when he saw that Parker was denied entry into carriage seven before the door into the next vestibule closed between them.

They reached the door, and instinctively tried to peer through the one-way glass, which would only be possible from the opposite direction unfortunately. To forestall a negative impression of him, from Parker or the other passengers, Will considerately knocked on the door while Milo cleared the nearest few rows of passengers for their safety. Cornering a combat veteran often has unpredictable consequences.

"Corporal Darius Parker! We know you're in there; the next car is on lock down. We also know that you never should've been in this situation in the first place. Come with us, quietly, and we promise to do what we can so that you're treated fairly."

They awaited a response but none came. Aside from what Milo assumed was general train noise, the entire carriage was silent. Suddenly, a loud mechanical 'clang' came from inside the vestibule. Parker was tinkering with *something*, and based on how the train ride was going thus far, they knew they had to go in. They each took a side, to cover the opposite end of the vestibule diagonally, and Milo hit the button to open the door, as well as activating a maintenance switch to prop it open.

Parker was filling the closed doorway to car seven, and had a mostly calm countenance about him. His right hand was on a strand of loose wires, while his left held white knuckled on to a handle that was present outside of every car. The only thing that gave away his anxiety of the situation was his wide eyes, which were especially apparent in the dark space.

"Ok Parker," Will began gently. "We're not with BOP or Rosen. What you've been accused of didn't warrant going to Leavenworth, and we have no intention of sending you back there if we can help it. Please, stop what you're doing and allow us to bring you in. There will be police at every station on this line, and they won't be as accommodating as we will."

Darius's eyes relaxed some, but his demeanor remained tense. "I didn't do anything wrong," he said in what Milo recognized as a south Chicago accent. "I had prescription meds, from my *doctor*, and I wasn't even driving! I was in a Johnny Cab!"

Both Milo and Will nodded at the statement. The Johnson Cab Company used automated taxis that had a robotic head and torso for the appearance of a real driver. They creeped Milo out, but they didn't seem to bother those who had no interest in conversation during their commute. Their fares were competitive with ride-share companies, so he understood their utility, but the couple of times he'd ridden in one all he did was stare at the 'driver,' which triggered an uncomfortable automated response.

"Sounds like an even worse deal than what Hyde was taken in for," Will blurted out, immediately regretting it.

Parker's wide-eyed expression seemed to bore into Will. "What happened with Hyde? Is he all right?" He asked as his frantic state ebbed back up.

Milo tried to salvage the conversation while Will composed himself. "We had convinced him to come with us to the US Marshal Field Office in Denver, but our mutual friends with Corrections took him before we could get there. We don't want that to happen to you. We're nearly to Salt Lake City. I have some colleagues who can help protect you, if you'll let us..."

Milo stopped talking when he saw Darius look down and stop paying attention. His mien became noticeably grim.

"I'm not going down like that," Darius muttered. "I didn't want to believe him, but Watson was being straight with us. I'm not going down like that," he repeated.

At that moment, Milo realized what the jumble of wires in Parker's hand were for. Darius intended to separate the train while he was between cars!

"Parker, you don't have to do this. Separating the train at this speed in a pressurized environment will end you, and possibly hurt innocent people as well. Do the honorable thing here and come with us, *please*!"

Darius looked up at both men; tears welling in his eyes. His stance relaxed slightly and he took his left hand off the handle it once firmly grasped. "Is that how you persuaded Hyde to come with you, before you let them take him to his death?"

Neither man had a response. Will saw Darius inhale deeply and yelled for him to wait, but he yanked down on the wire bundle with relative ease, and his pleas were drowned out by the howling wind and screams from passengers.

An alarm claxon sounded overhead, and there was a rush of cold air beckoning them to the door, as well as any loose items within the carriage, as the pressure tried to rapidly equalize. Before the door that now lead to the chilly autumn afternoon air slammed shut in front of Will and Milo, as it was programmed to do in such emergencies, they witnessed Parker's body get whisked away like fallen leaves in a gust of wind.

With the door now closed, a muted unrest filled the train, aside from the occasional confused murmur and nervous whimper. Milo and Will paid no attention to them though. They were so paralyzed by Parker's sacrifice they couldn't rouse enough strength to pick themselves off the maroon-carpeted floor, or even raise their heads. Moments later, an automated announcement, with a soft female voice, said in three languages that they were about to arrive into Salt Lake City, and for everyone to take their seats. Milo and Will didn't move.

Chapter Seven: Showtime

The hover train was behind schedule for its arrival at the Salt Lake City station. It slowed to allow the five disconnected cars to reattach, but when the relinking was completed it was only a few minutes later than normal. Milo extracted his car from the train before it continued its trek west, and he and Will remained at the station to file their reports and figure out their next move.

Response teams from the local police agencies and the National Transportation Safety Board had yet to locate Parker's body. Milo was on his secure mobile, checking in with Kirlan to inquire if any of the other teams had any status updates on the final fugitive. As he predicted, all of the work on the so-called 'Task Force Rubicon' continued to come from one team; his.

Will was back on his flex tablet. His fingers were a blur as they danced over the display screen. It reminded Milo of a marionette show he saw as a child; the same one he took his own children to when they were the same age he had been when he watched it. The two men hadn't interacted with each other for the last forty minutes, and Milo was ready to shake more answers out him.

"What do you think Parker meant when he said 'Watson was straight with us?' What did Watson know that the others didn't?"

Will suddenly froze where he sat, his hand hovering over his tablet. "It was believed, by someone above my paygrade, that Watson was the original target of Rosen. The prevailing rumor was that he was approached by someone who made him an offer to join the Most Dangerous Game's team of hunters. Following that alleged meeting, he disappeared for three days while on mission for the Agency in Belarus."

Milo was amazed by Will's candor. He wasn't sure which piece of information to comment on to keep the tentative communications door open, so he went for the most obvious choice. "Since we're talking in hypotheticals here, what's the current theory on his little hiatus then?"

Will rolled up his tablet and sat back in his train station bench. Milo was amused to witness the man put his hand on his chin the same way he did when deep in thought. "If anybody knows that little tidbit, they haven't told me. But my guess is that Watson accepted their offer but changed his mind at some point, so he tried to shake them and didn't report in. Rosen of course took care of the rest, making sure he'd find his way to BOP once he turned up."

"That's a very compelling story," Milo countered cynically as he took a break from pacing and sat down next to Will, "but how did two additional spec ops vets get roped into this master plan as well? Wrong place, wrong time I gather?"

Will stood up and stretched. He started at his neck, went to his shoulders and arms, then rotated his hips in a very methodical fashion. The impressively fluid way in which he moved seemed to Milo that either Will had spent a lot of time in the field, or he had some medical training, or possibly both.

"I'm still working on that," Will said with a sigh. "I wonder if there's anything to eat around here. I'm famished."

"Right," Milo agreed as he stood up as well, knowing the conversation was over for the moment. They gathered their things and went to retrieve the Studebaker. It took the auto-valet far longer than it should have, considering there weren't many cars in the older-style garage to begin with. There were other places closer to the train station, but neither of them had been to Salt Lake City before, so they asked around as to what the good restaurants were. R&R BBQ came highly recommended.

~

For the second time that day, the person in the black Citroën watched as the now familiar Studebaker lifted off and drifted away. This time however, she had no idea where they were going. The pair of federal investigators was far more adept than she gave them credit for. Not only had they deduced who had helped the three veterans in an impressive amount of time, they were also able to quickly figure out that the airport was not a viable means of escape and somehow got onboard the hyper-train before it reached its next major stop.

Within six hours, give or take, her plan had gone down the proverbial toilet. Hyde wasn't interested in her proposal in the least, and he assured her that he would be safe with the Isard girl for at least a few days. That should've been plenty of time for the plan to be concluded, and the other two didn't want to push him, nor did they have the time to do so. Parker, on the other hand, agreed to the terms he was given, but wanted to follow through with them from a location that involved less personal risk. This was the reason she was parked in the standard train station parking lot, awaiting his arrival. They adjusted their strategy in order to bring him to people he could trust. How devastating it was for all involved to learn that Parker had likely not survived their escape plan, and the means in which it had happened. The show must go on, she convinced herself, and listlessly drove off as if even her car was in mourning.

~

They arrived at the restaurant before the bustle of an evening crowd, so they were seated right away. The interior appeared to not know what it wanted to be; a southern steakhouse or a sports bar. No matter which way someone interpreted the place, the fragrance from the meats and spices were intoxicating. Milo's stomach growled within seconds of sitting down.

Will was quick to order a brisket sandwich and one of the local beers, while Milo went with the pulled chicken, with one of their spicier sauces, and an Arnold Palmer to wash it down. Their drinks came quickly, with the awkwardness settling in shortly afterward. They had been in each other's company for nearly ten hours, but they still didn't know much about one another. There were so many questions Milo wanted to ask Will, but they were all related to the case and he wanted a reprieve from that for a while. Milo took a sip of his drink and decided to break the ice.

"So," Milo began hesitantly. "What were you doing before you signed up with CID? Did you get any relatable training before then?"

Will was drinking his beer so heartily that Milo's question seemed to catch him completely off guard. He finished the drink in two more large gulps, then gave Milo a look like he had forgotten he was there.

"Yes, well... Um, after the war, I went to medical school, you see. I was looking for work as a medical doctor when I learned my talents could be useful elsewhere."

Will paused a moment to order another beer before continuing. "What about you? You seem more cut out for a military investigator than I am. What made you go for the Marshals?"

Milo watched, mildly impressed, as Will downed half his second beer as if he were a pledge at a frat house, or a sailor on shore leave. He looked at his half-and-half iced tea lemonade, slowly being diluted by melting ice, and considered ordering a beer as well. If his decades of military training and experience taught him anything it was to avoid alcohol while on duty, so he ultimately decided against it.

"Quite simple really. The Army had been part of my life for so long I couldn't think of anything beyond its reach. So I let my wife decide. She'd put up with enough of my moving around and whatnot, I figured it was her turn to steer the ship, so to speak. One of her six sisters had moved to Chicago alone the year before and wanted some familial company. My CO knew someone high up in the Marshals Service and recommended me. I was able to split the last six months of my fourth enlistment while I trained for the Service, as well as choose my duty station when I completed both."

Will chugged the rest of his beer and wiped his mouth on his sleeve. "Sounds like a cozy transition. Too bad more vets separating from service don't experience that." He paused, and considered the hundreds of vets who aren't so lucky. "Married huh? Any kids?"

"Kids? No. I have twin teenage daughters who think they're thirty. Sometimes I'm surprised to come home to see them there because they could probably get a job that easily earns more than my wife and I make together and move to a bigger place... Seriously though, they're good kids and they make their parents proud every day. I just wish they had a little more ambition; not too much though. You?"

"Yeah. A son. Just turned nine a couple months ago. I can't imagine my life without him. You're still relatively young and in good shape right? I can barely keep up with my son as it is. I don't want to think about how much trouble teenage girls can get into. But I suppose there is a double standard with that sort of thing."

The first genuine conversation between them was cut short by the arrival of their late lunch, or early dinner; however one looked at it. Like his beer, Will devoured his mountain of a sandwich as if he hadn't eaten in days. Milo looked on in amazement, wondering how this could be the same man who was just speaking fondly about children less than a minute prior. He shook his head and started in, as Will was already halfway done. Milo had only taken a few bites when some commotion in the bar area grabbed their attention.

Suspended above the bar, projected by dozens of holographic emitters, was the all-too-familiar opening title song for The Most Dangerous Game. Several patrons of the restaurant were hooting and hollering as the line-up of hunters was announced. Next was the introduction of the runner. The image of a man labeled as Prisoner 74205 was displayed with some stats scrolling between still pictures and video clips of him performing various actions. Watching the scenes publicizing some of the man's physical prowess and weapons skills got the growing crowd abuzz, but all Milo and Will could do was exchange pensive looks. The mocha-skinned young man preparing to participate in a contest for his life was none other than Marcus Hyde.

"Damn," Milo muttered loudly. "They sure didn't waste any time getting him suited up, did they?" Will just shook his head in shame. Milo knew exactly what he was thinking; if only they had reached him sooner, or exited out the back door instead...

The transport from Rosen headquarters in Reno, Nevada touched down on the pad at Zone Jupiter; aptly named due to its size and inhospitable sub-regions compared to the other proving grounds. The pad began to lower into the underground caverns that were once silver mines, and the still growing restaurant crowd went wild.

Hyde was out of the transport craft and geared-up as the pad approached the halfway point. He leapt off before the descending lift reached the bottom and sprinted away from the pad through the maze of tunnels that made up one of the sub-regions of Zone Jupiter. While the mine was once a thriving network when in operation, it had since gone into disrepair and was sealed off for a time well over a century ago. Then Rosen purchased the land, and they didn't hesitate to reopen it, following a rushed clean-up operation that likely cost more than the land was worth.

As a decorated Colonial Cavalier, who helped secure and protect some of the fledgling interstellar colonies during his three tours off planet, being in cramped, underground environments was like second nature to Hyde. His speed and efficiency moving around the caverns would make one think he had lived there most of his life. He rounded another corner, not hesitating to choose which route to take when faced with forks in the aging tunnel system, and deftly avoided the various hazards along the way; both natural and manmade.

Suddenly, he stopped. The dozens of hidden cameras cycled through the claustrophobic space until they found the best angle to show him tinkering with something. "Looks like he's taking apart a seeker," Milo said curiously, stopping his hand midway to his chin. He instead grabbed his glass and took a drink to resist that urge.

In seconds Hyde had removed a piece of one of his seekers, and stuffed the remaining component into a gouge of the crumbling rock wall. Only about ten seconds had passed since he paused in the tunnel. Now he had turned around to explore another shaft of rock, and place a second neutered seeker probe.

"Brilliant," Milo declared. "He removed the propulsion system, so they don't move around and give themselves away. They'll still transmit, but the hunter won't be able to detect them as easily. He's creating his own security grid, inside a tunnel system he'd presumably never been in before." Will nodded at the remark but didn't take his eyes off the show.

Hyde entered a larger chamber, which looked to be the mine's ore processing center, with some fairly modern pieces of machinery thrown in to give the appearance it was still functioning. He clipped the proverbial wings of two more seekers, placing them in strategic locations around the space, and did a quick recon of the cavern. He quickly progressed around the space, studying some of the machinery, and found a partially protected hiding place that had a nearly full view of the area.

He took a moment to relax a bit, providing the production team a perfect opportunity to advertise some sponsors, but it was far too short a reprieve for anyone to get comfortable. Hyde had just finished a fruit-oat protein bar, with its logo clearly visible for all to see, when his forearm display, presented on the left of the main viewing area, was pinged. Something, or someone had set off one of his passive seekers.

Hyde readied himself for action by shifting around his gear for maximum offensive efficiency. Seconds stretched slowly by. Everyone in the restaurant was on the edge of their seat with baited breath. A full minute passed. People began to return to their meal or drinks, as well as breathe, when there was definitive movement at the other end of the vast, underground chamber. The eatery became so quiet, the slightest shift from anyone could be noticed from opposite ends of the dining area. On impulse, everyone began to lean forward as cameras began to zoom in on a nondescript corner.

Chapter Eight: Cautionary Tale

Cameras from around the cavern came to life as a dark figure crept out of the shadows. The dim, dated light fixtures did a fine job of maintaining the intruder's anonymity, but once his attire was glimpsed, everyone who had even a small level of show knowledge knew who it was.

The imposing figure of a burly man was evident even in the poor visibility, but what really gave Hunter McCone away was his trademark helmet and flight jacket. The brass-colored, green lens helmet looked like something out of the early-to-mid twentieth century. The brown leather jacket may have had an even older design, but neither were what they seemed.

The helmet, an homage to one of his father's favorite movies as a child, held the latest in audio/visual technology. Any noise, no matter how faint, would be instantly identified. If its sophisticated internal system failed to identify the sound, a catalogued list of the top three likely sources would be displayed. The large, emerald green lenses were sensitive enough to detect unnatural disruptions in air movement, as well as many other features, including of course a high level of protection from physical impacts.

Elad McCone was recruited into the hunter fold shortly after his performance in quelling the food riots in the Disney Region of California as a lieutenant in the state's Governors Police Bureau. His aggressive, tactical command decisions that left dozens dead and many more wounded, were quietly praised by some officials in the state capital, but very publicly decried as a level of unprecedented and unnecessary brutality.

His days as a law enforcer over, he quickly made a name for himself as a new hunter yet to receive more than a skinned knee during the Game. As a small irony, he was given a specially designed riot shotgun as his primary weapon, a choice he claims he wouldn't have made if the network's production team wasn't so insistent. McCone grew to respect the weapon however, due to its versatility and ease of switching between the impressive variety of shells it was loaded with, depending what the situation called for.

The reputation he earned was prevalent as he lurked in the shadows, growing the excitement in the now crowded barbeque restaurant. Projected over the bar, his silhouette waded into the rocky cavern with caution and precision; scanning sections of the chamber efficiently and methodically. He felt confident enough to venture farther into the room, but froze in place next to a piece of machinery: an old ore processor, one that Hyde had manipulated for a few seconds. McCone went in for a closer look at the control panel, and the cameras zoomed in on Hyde tapping carefully on his forearm computer pad.

The control panel exploded with a blinding flash of light. Although he was in no physical danger, McCone instinctively covered his face with his arm until his helmet's sensory filters activated and his eyes could readjust to dusk-lit space. As fast as they were, the filters weren't as fast as Marcus Hyde.

Before McCone brought his arm back down, Hyde was upon him. The lithe younger man slammed his shoulder into the hulk-like body of his opponent with all his might. McCone was caught completely off guard and toppled onto the old conveyor belt. Since the incendiary bomb Hyde made from a seeker probe propulsion cell destroyed the controls, the conveyor wasn't going to be moving anytime soon. Instead, Hyde pulled the pin out of a grenade attached to the flaying man's left pant leg, and then he ran down the passageway McCone had just entered from.

The restaurant Milo and Will were in was now packed to capacity. The din of the crowd steadily grew and was close to a fever pitch by that point. Even the serving staff was caught up in the spectacle, as orders were piling up on the monitor by the serving window, which offered a glimpse into the kitchen.

Much to the crowd's satisfaction, McCone came to his senses soon enough to grab the active grenade and throw it safely across the cavern before it exploded. He got to his feet in a jolt, scanned the room briefly, and then chased after Hyde like a bloodhound following a scent.

Some of the virtual spectators in the restaurant were arguing about why Marcus didn't try to shoot McCone while he was down and disoriented. Others defended him by pointing out the quality of hunters' body armor. And a pair of business men, recently off work judging by their relaxed dark-blue suits, claimed it was a ploy to boost ratings the longer the match lasted. Milo simply rolled his eyes and Will shook his head at the insipid conversation.

Hyde was running full speed through the tunnel. No one in the eatery, aside from Milo and Will, seemed to be impressed by Marcus moving as fast as he was while carrying what they estimated as thirty kilos of gear on him. Milo didn't want to hold his breath, but he was beginning to think Hyde may be able to stay ahead of McCone for a while. Though much like the tortoise and the hare, slow and steady could very well win the race. He knew in situations like these, it all came down to wit and cunning.

Marcus came to a fork in the tunnel system once again and didn't hesitate in choosing the left path. Four paces in and he stopped jarringly. Hyde walked tentatively back to the other path, knowing full well that McCone was getting closer by the second, and casually walked the other direction he just bypassed a minute prior.

"Prisoner 74205 may have just made a fatal mistake, ladies and gentlemen," lead PR announcer Joram Bachman shared. "That path is what the hunters call the 'tunnel of doom' due to its many pitfalls and cave-ins."

The eatery had fallen tensely quiet as everyone watched Hyde struggle around boulders and debris from centuries-old mining operations. McCone paused for a brief instant, and then agitatedly took the right tunnel in pursuit of Hyde. It appeared to Milo that his shoulders slumped some when he realized his quarry had gone that direction. Perhaps hunters were made aware of their terrain beforehand, he mused.

Minutes drifted away and Hyde seemed to be getting somewhat apprehensive. Milo wondered if Marcus was regretting his chosen path, because the terrain was slowing him down immensely. The next obstacle however, garnered a devious glint in his eyes that was shockingly clear plastered on the screens and projectors of the bar.

Marcus approached a large fissure in the rocky ground. He peered down into the abyss beyond with his wrist light and saw nothing but darkness. Hyde dove into his gear bag and furiously searched inside. After a few seconds, he apparently found what he was looking for and tossed the bag to the opposite side of the chasm. He carefully placed something on each side of the tunnel, just before the perilous breach, and leapt over, grabbing his gear and continuing his flight down the path.

As Hyde turned the corner, out of frame, the camera zoomed in on the crevice slowly. Then it disappeared into the rock like it wasn't there at all. The crowd gasped, muttering and arguing what had happened. Will gave Milo a knowing look and smile. Marcus had placed an adaptive camouflage expander by the hole. Designed for defensive purposes, it was typically used to hide people from attack, or equipment from plunder. Hyde was using his ACE to conceal a probable fatal hazard.

The camera angle changed to show McCone drifting around the bend, quickly but vigilantly like a wraith. Some of the restaurant patrons shouted out warnings, as if they thought the man could hear them from nearly eight-hundred kilometers away, which made Will slowly turn his head to give them a look of derision. Strangely enough however, the scattered pleas appeared to have been answered.

McCone's hurried pace came to a skidding halt mere centimeters from the chasm. He scanned the area very thoroughly, deciding whether to trust his senses, or the very sensitive audio/visual readouts in his helmet. He probed around by tossing some stones and crept closer to the fissure.

He neared what was assumed to be the edge and visibly relaxed. The crowd followed suit. McCone began to search for the ACE when the right side of the tunnel exploded in a fireball of bright light and stone. The camera that had been active lost signal, so the angle shifted several times before settling on one at the opposite end of the crevice. This camera looked no better than the previous though; the view was still too dark and smoky to identify anything, except more rock.

It took what felt like several minutes for the smoke to clear enough to process the scene. Once it did, several gasps rang out in unison at the sight of the noticeably larger hole in the ground, with no McCone to be seen. Curses and praises alike rang out in the eatery directed at Marcus, but Milo and Will sat as serenely as statues still taking in the spectacle they had just witnessed.

In the few seconds Hyde rummaged through his gear bag, he had managed to also grab a proximity mine, and likely any remaining seeker batteries to combine them into an extra-lethal bomb. Camouflaged by the ACE, McCone was bound to fall victim to one or the other. His demise was inevitable, though probably not in the literal blaze of glory most wanted or expected.

The picture changed to a disheveled but steadfast Marcus Hyde emerging from the infamous 'tunnel of doom' into a cave with some natural light. He looked up to see a network drone hovering over him, which garnered a heavy sigh in response.

"Prisoner 74205, you have just felled an experienced and celebrated hunter. To what do you attribute your victory?" The smooth voice of Joram Bachman from the gaming headquarters asked through the drone's speakers.

Hyde stared at the drone with a life-sized image of Bachman projected in front of him with extreme contempt. It was obvious Marcus didn't want to even look at the man, let alone converse with him. He knew however that if he didn't respond there would be repercussions in the form of fewer aid drops, advancement to less desirable locations, and better prepared hunters.

"Training, and instinct. Along with a bit of luck, I suppose," he answered in his slow southern drawl.

"Very encouraging young man," Bachman bantered. "Is there anything you'd like to say to your growing number of fans out there?"

Marcus gave the camera a very hard look. "Yeah, I do believe there is. Freedom is only real when you fight for it. As the sun makes its zenith, so must I."

The camera angle changed and the drone could be seen drifting away, out of frame. Marcus composed himself and continued his trek into the waning sunlight. The restaurant was beginning to clear out, while the game master prattled on about how Hyde had nearly twelve hours until his next match. Amongst the maelstrom of departing customers Milo and Will remained seated, too stunned to move.

"So what do you suppose he meant by that last line, 'the sun making its zenith...' something or other?" Will asked in a profound tone to a much quieter establishment.

"I don't know," Milo breathed as he stood up, after settling the bill. "Maybe Watson can tell us, *once* we find him. What do you say we refocus on that, eh?"

"Ok, sounds good. Any idea where to start? Our teams at the airport didn't come up with anything. We are officially out of leads."

"Really? There's nothing in that magical tablet of yours?" Milo rejoined with a smirk as they both got in the car. "Well, there's obviously an interest in Rosen's connection with our fugitives, particularly by Watson. Not to mention Hyde's suspicious appearance on their show so quickly after the escape and capture, by *us*," he added with disappointed emphasis. "How about we knock on their door? For all we know, Watson could've been on that same train as well, and it probably passed through Reno not too long ago... Then again, maybe it *has* been a while; I already forgot how fast that train moves. Not sure how something like that could slip my mind so soon. What?"

He looked over to see Will staring at him agape; a first by Milo's reckoning. "By jove, I think you may be onto something! What better way to make us think that they had split up than to merely separate temporarily? Parker was no slouch, that's for sure, but Watson has *considerably* more training and experience at making himself invisible. We could've easily walked right past him in pursuit of Parker and not even known it. Ok, I'm sold. Let's head over to the 'Biggest Little City in America.' I bet that it's twenty percent bigger since the last time I've used that phrase," he concluded, laughing at his own joke.

Chapter Nine: Life Lessons

Footage of Prisoner 74205's inspired performance played for the third time on Sonya's home entertainment system. She'd never been the type to have the best home system money could buy. Her training and production manager from the company had talked her into going big, in case she wanted to impress guests or host events at her house. Over six years and counting, she still had yet to have any guests; ones who weren't work-related anyway.

When the company put her up in a cabin at Lake Tahoe, quickly approaching a decade ago, she didn't recall reading in her contract that her social life, what little there was to begin with, had come to an end. Sure, she'd had people over on occasion for one-night stands and the like, but she still considered that work-related as they had always been with colleagues. It was difficult to make new friends in her line of work. People either annoyingly fawned over her celebrity status, or were repelled by it.

If she'd known signing with Rosen would've effectively made her a hermit, she would've listened to her former company commander and applied to Officer Candidate School. Sonya didn't feel she was ready, or qualified, to get a commission in the Marines, but Captain Bates insisted she was. Uncertainty unfortunately won that stalemate.

Sonya was about to turn off the replay of the match when she paused the image. Right after the bomb exploded, although he had picked up his pace and was already a few hundred meters away, 74205 lowered his head in a seemingly respectful bow. Not only that, the regret that poured from his face and body language was palpable. For the first time in longer than she could remember, Sonya found herself in tears.

The loss of yet another colleague was only part of the catalyst for her extraordinary emotional response. She hadn't been close to Elad. Their meetings were seldom more than the occasional bump into at the training room over the years, outside of the fan-favorite hunter team-ups however. She had a professional respect for the man, but felt he was one of the only people who actually *belonged* in that line of work.

She was surprised to admit that the bulk of her grief was toward the young man who completely outsmarted an experienced hunter. Someone whose background and crimes she was entirely oblivious to. An honorable man she didn't know, who she will likely be tasked to 'instill justice upon,' as the Network liked to put it. That's who was at the forefront of her lapse in carefully conditioned mood levels, through the help of years of trauma therapy and psychotropic medication.

Sonya had inquired about the background and charges of contestants twice in the past. Both times her manager discouraged her from seeking such information as it could "affect your resolve in carrying out your duties." At the time she understood a certain level of moral buffering between her and her targets, but her recent victories made her rethink where her comfort zone actually stood.

She ordered her phone to call her manager, but before she realized what she wanted to say, Suresh had picked up the line and was beaming at her with that blindingly white, toothy smile of his.

"Sonya!" He energetically greeted her. "To what do I owe the pleasure of this unexpected call?"

Timir Suresh was a tall, thin, and impeccably groomed Indian man from South Africa. Sonya thought he would make an excellent politician, if he wasn't so in love with being in, or right next to, the spotlight so much. She had never seen him romantically involved with anyone; man or woman. Throughout all the time they spent together, Suresh had neither made a pass at her, nor given off any hints or vibes that he was gay. Eventually, Sonya assumed that he simply fancied himself, and that was enough for the both of them to understand each other it seemed.

"I know what you're going to say Timmy," a name he allowed only a select few people to use, "but I want to know what our current contestant is charged with. It's also apparent he's had some military or police training. I'd like info on that as well."

Timir sighed, his smile dimming some. "You're right Sonya. We've been over this before. It's not your job to get to know these people. In fact, I'd argue that it would be counter-productive for you to do so."

Sonya knew he was right, but she did her best not to show it. "Yes we have Timmy, but this time is different. He seems awfully young, with a sense of fair play, to be some master criminal. Secondly, if I'm being asked to put down another veteran I'd like to at least know a little about his training to better grasp his motivations."

Suresh's smile faded completely, and he took on a scolding look. "You aren't *asked* to put down anyone, Sonya. It's your *job* to retire criminals efficiently and without prejudice. While I doubt much could affect your efficiency, I have concerns that giving you this information will affect your performance, in one way or another."

She attempted to mimic his condescending look. "I'm a big girl Timmy. And I've been doing this almost as long as you. All I'm asking for are his charges and where he received his specialized training, assuming he's not just magically gifted that is."

A minute-long, intense stare-down followed. Eventually, Timir sat back in his seat and looked away to his left. "I'll see what I can find and get back to you."

"We both know you can look up that info in a second, if you haven't committed it to memory already," she countered, not backing down.

Another pause. "Fine," he submitted. "He's been accused of rape, and he's spent some time with the Colonial Cavalry," he finished sheepishly.

She stared at Suresh openmouthed. "*Accused!* You mean he hasn't been convicted or sentenced yet?"

"This is *exactly* what I've been trying to avoid all these years. It's already clear to me that your tenacity has been compromised. Perhaps I'm misremembering the verbiage, or that's simply the way it was detailed in the report. I don't work for the Justice Department, and neither do you. But I think we both understand how the particulars in terminology can be taken out of context unintentionally. I didn't give it a second thought, and I don't think *anyone* else should either."

"Nothing on my end has been compromised, Timmy. I'm not so sure about you though. Your point is well taken about legal lingo, but that doesn't sound like a mistake someone who writes arrest and prosecution reports would make. How did he even get on our radar in the first place if he hasn't been through the system yet?"

"If you must know," Timir answered in a pompous tone, "he escaped from custody before he could answer for his crime. Apparently, when he was caught, somebody above both of our paygrades thought sending him to us was both legal and justified. That's good enough for me, and therefore should be for you."

That revelation changed things somewhat in Sonya's mind, but she didn't like the shift in Suresh's demeanor. He had always been protective of her, in a smarmy way, but he had never talked down to her the way he was presently doing, and she wasn't about to let him off easy.

"Okay," she annunciated slowly. "Good to know. You said he spent time with the Colonial Cavalry. What does that mean? Was he part of the Lunar or Martian conflicts? And this time, try to tell me without the attitude if you please."

Timir was looking downright annoyed at that point, but after a moment of contemplation he seemed to lighten up some. "Actually, which participating conflicts, if any, were not revealed to the Network. If memory serves, that type of information is withheld until after a subject is retired. Having said that," he continued abashedly once more, "I do recall reading that he had earned a bronze star."

Great, Sonya thought. Not only was he a kid, who may or may not be guilty of a serious crime, and forced into a literal game of life or death, but he's also a war hero. Though she wasn't sure, she had strong suspicions that her previous target of the day before had combat experience as well.

"Thank you very much Timmy, you've been most helpful. I'm sure that intel will be useful in the inevitable likelihood I'll be tasked to hunt this young man."

Suresh composed himself back to his normal façade. "There's no guarantee that you will land this case Sonya. He has to survive the second round before the final challenger, and that isn't always the chief hunter. It'll be whomever the Network deems most expected to entice the largest audience and sponsorship. Another part of your contract you should be well aware of."

It was Sonya's turn to be patronizing. "Trust me Timmy. By the way he handled McCone, and the scraps of data you just provided me, both the viewers and producers alike will be clamoring for *me*."

With that last bout of self-confidence, she ended the call as he prepared a rebuttal. She was confused and frustrated by the whole situation; feelings she wasn't used to having. For the first time since the war, she found herself genuinely afraid. The confusing part was not knowing if that fear was due to her facing off with an equally shrewd opponent, or not knowing if doing so was even justified. That rare insecurity was quite perplexing to her.

Sonya allowed those thoughts and feelings to consume her, culminating with the realization that she had no one to turn to for help. She had cut herself off from her friends and family years ago, due either to fame or disapproval of her career choice; probably an equal combination of both. She also couldn't trust anyone at the Network, since they'd likely have the same reaction as Timir's miniature meltdown.

After long moments of deliberation, and increasing feelings of seclusion, Sonya landed on the one person she knew she could still count on to be straightforward with her without judgement. Although she may have to endure a few barbs about not signing on with OCS, Sonya was confident her former company commander would know what she should do, or at least point her in the right direction.

She did a double take when her computer informed her that Captain Bates was not only still in the Marines, but had evidently gotten married and also been promoted to lieutenant colonel. The all too familiar video ComNet banner of the Defense Department appeared around a smiling woman by the name of Lindsey Dune. To Sonya, it seemed she hadn't aged a day.

"Good morning Colonel," Sonya said, dropping the lieutenant in acceptable fashion. "Do you have a minute for an 'I told you so?'"

Chapter Ten: Alias

Milo and Will were back in the Sky Hawk and on their way to Reno. Milo was checking in with his supervisor, while Will was fighting, and failing, to stay awake. The one thing keeping him from falling completely asleep was the relentless chirping of his flex tablet. Milo weighed his options in trying to help, knowing it probably wouldn't lead anywhere; but he felt he should try nonetheless.

"Despite popular belief, tablets, or any computer really, can be turned off. I don't even need all these dash displays on, now that I think about it. They're supposed to be aides, not something to be dependent on for every little thing." Monitors and applications on the heads-up display, or HUD, began winking off one by one, making the space as dark as the twilight outside. Will opened his mouth in protest, but his clear fatigue made him rethink the gesture. Besides, Will seemed less bothered by the device.

Milo was sure his passenger was out when one of Will's other devices started making a different noise. Milo caught a glimpse of Will's watch, and it appeared he was getting a call. Will groggily turned his wrist to read the display and sat bolt upright.

"Uh oh," Milo chided, "this one must be important."

"It's my wife," Will said as he mussed his hair and rubbed his eyes, making them more red than they were before.

"That'd be a big yes."

Will unrolled his tablet across his lap and transferred the call to it. "Hey Lin. What did I forget?"

Milo looked over briefly at the screen and saw a strikingly lovely woman, with dark hair wrapped tightly in a bun. He snuck another look out of shock after noticing she was a lieutenant colonel in the Marines.

"Nothing, as far as I know. But I'll keep looking," Lindsey Dune answered with a wry grin, barely braking her playful, yet steel visage. "You'll never guess who I just talked to."

Will gave her a knowing smile. He was very good at this game. He had been right far more often than not when she asked this question. Right now however, between being roused from much-needed sleep, and getting assigned a very absorbing case at the last minute, he didn't have the energy to commit to a sincere level.

"Uh... hm. You caught me off guard Lin. Um, General Regulus? He's ready to give you another promotion, because you like birds better than oak leaves? Or better yet, wondering when you're going to retire, so you stop making everyone else look bad," he responded expectantly.

"I can see that you're exhausted, so I'll let this one slide," she said still smiling. "Believe it or not, Sonya Kane just contacted me out of the blue, after seven years."

Upon hearing that name, Milo couldn't help taking a longer look at the woman on the glowing display on Will's lap. When he returned to the piloting controls he noticed their speed and trajectory needed to be readjusted. Not that he was enamored with the woman, but he couldn't believe the coincidence of

Sonya's name coming up when she may be culpable in the dozen crimes her employers are accused of.

"Oh? How does she know *you*?"

"I'm sure I told you this before, but I was her lieutenant at one point; on some of our more interesting missions... Or was I a captain by then?" She paused a moment, deep in thought. "Eh, doesn't matter. Anyway, she wanted some of my sage advice... she always was such a smart girl to ask," she said as her grin grew.

"After a short bit of reminiscing, she wondered if I could get her any data on the current Game contestant; the one who apparently won in ingenious fashion..."

"Why would she ask *you* for that?" Will interjected. "She probably has an army of people at her beck and call."

She gave him a scolding look. "I'm getting to that, dear. Apparently, they keep her on such a tight leash that she doesn't trust a lot of the people she works with. So, she reached out to the *one* person she knew she could trust," Lindsey concluded with a prideful grin. Will couldn't resist the urge of rolling his eyes, and made sure Lindsey saw.

He gave her a moment before continuing. He knew one of her regrets was that she didn't have many female friends; working in very much still a predominantly male profession. "Ok. That's nice. But it doesn't really answer why she would think you would have access to that information."

"Honestly, I don't think she actually did. She was simply looking for someone to reach out to," Lindsey answered morosely. "But as it happens, I was certain this was something that falls into your area of expertise. Without giving her any specifics, or making any promises, I told her I'd inquire on her behalf. I know that you're working on a case right now, but if you can help her with this dilemma just say the word. Otherwise, you can disavow any knowledge of this conversation."

Will stared at her in utter shock. He couldn't believe the incredible opportunity this presented. He looked over at Milo in disbelief, and the man gave him an impatient nod with tented eye brows. They were on their way to persuade someone with Rosen to let them poke around, a tactic that was sure to fail. A chance meeting like the one that had just fallen into his lap may have salvaged the entire trip.

"As crazy as this sounds Lin, the case I'm working is directly related to Sonya's employers. We're headed to their headquarters in Reno now in a futile bid to squeeze answers out of them, but we'd *much* rather talk with her first... For purely professional reasons of course," he conceded wryly.

"We?" She probed succinctly.

"Ah, yes, my current partner in crime; Deputy US Marshal Milo Durron. He was kind enough to do the driving, in his snazzy new Studebaker."

"So *that's* why you're not cranky! You convinced him to drive?" she chided, the smile returning in full force. "Well, if that wasn't serendipitous enough for you, she lives in the Tahoe area. I'll connect back with her and message you where she wants to meet."

"Thanks Lin. We couldn't have done it without you, and likely wouldn't have either. How's Sean?"

"He's fine; misses his dad though. I'd put him on but he's in his homework groove at the moment. Who knows how long it would take to get him back there if I were to interrupt now. You two be careful, starting with not pissing off Sonya," she concluded sternly."

After their goodbyes, Will switched his tablet back off, returning the car to its early evening lighting in the process. A few minutes passed with him beaming a content grin. Then, like an afterthought, he snapped his head toward Milo to finally ask if he minded making a slight detour. Milo shook his head piteously.

"I was wondering if you were going to ask, or just assume I'd be ok with a backseat driver. Well lucky for you the answer is I don't mind. It'd be pretty stupid of us *not* to meet with her… but there's just one caveat."

Will gave him a confused look. "Ok," he droned suspiciously.

"Tell me your real name, and who you really work for so I don't have to waste time looking it up myself."

Will's mien changed from one of confusion to wide-eyed panic. He turned and looked out the window in a robotic manner. "I believe that's actually two caveats," came the pithy rejoinder, eventually.

"I saw your wife's uniform; who looks lovely in camo by the way. Her rank, service patch, and name tape were clearly visible. It wouldn't be much of a job to find info on a Lieutenant Colonel Dune of the Marine Corps, a son named Sean, with a husband named…?"

Several seconds passed with Will remaining steadfast to the passenger window. After a full minute of Milo's bewildering stare, Will sighed and slumped in his plush seat some. After a few more moments of processing his options, he decided on the path of most resistance.

"My name is Harold Dune, but you can call me Hal... in private that is, until this mission is over. Or better yet, until I say it's ok," he finished with a bland smirk.

"That wouldn't be *doctor* Dune, would it? The man who helped expose Omnium Corps' less-than-scrupulous business practices? Who then pulled a Houdini trick shortly thereafter?"

Will mechanically turned his head back to face Milo. In what seemed to be outrage tempered by skepticism he asked, "you *know* about that? I thought my name was kept out of the media! The Bureau said they'd bury it after I made my statement to special counsel."

"That would be a first. Couldn't say if it was on the official documents shared with the public, but having just left active duty to work with the Marshals there's little chance a story about such egregious violations against veterans would escape my notice. I did some digging on the whole thing in my off hours. The Justice Department may not play well with others at times, but we do tend to impart well to each other internally when the need arises, and under optimal circumstances of course."

"Well, I guess Defense Intelligence isn't as thorough with their cover-ups as they claim," Hal conceded cynically. "That's who I work for by the way... to fulfill your second stipulation. I've been assigned to a highly exclusive team of three; me, some Department of Corrections trainer, and a handler of sorts. We specialize in criminal exploitation of military assets; both alive and inanimate."

"Alive and inanimate huh. That seems like a strange slogan," Milo bantered slyly. "How were you able to infiltrate Omnium so effectively? They're only now getting back on their feet from what I hear. There's no way they'll reach their pre-scandal reputation at this point though, or surpass their biggest competitor in Seattle."

"Oh, well, that was sheer dumb luck. I was an employee of theirs, legitimately. No infiltration required. A colleague tipped me off about some shady affairs, but by then I already had suspicions of my own. I had begun some rudimentary research on the company when I was approached by a pair of cops. That's when I got in a bit too deep. They recruited me, in a manner of speaking, and the whole event caught the eye of DIA. I suppose if I didn't have bad luck with that whole affair, I'd have no luck at all."

"And here you are again; doing the legwork without any arrest authority. That's why you need *me*, or someone with DOJ at least. Do I have that about right?"

"Oh come off it! This wasn't some grand scheme I put together. There *really* was a prison break, and there's a genuine search going on co-opted by the Marshals and CID. The escape is the only thing that's been orchestrated here, and I'd like to think you're starting to see that."

"That's quite an assumption coming from someone directing me from the passenger seat of my car, so he couldn't be tracked from his government issued National. Keeping me in the dark the whole way through I might add. You don't know me at all Will... or Hal... or whatever you want to call yourself. You don't want to be straight with me, fine. But it's a long walk back to civilization."

Hal opened his mouth to protest, until he saw the smirk creeping across Milo's face and shook his head exasperatedly. "Dammit man! Are you *ever* serious?"

Milo couldn't help chuckling. "Maybe I was wrong. Perhaps you do know me after all. Now what do you say we get back to it, and go meet the *deadly* serious Sonya at... do we have a location yet mister Bond?"

Hal ignored the joke and checked his messages. He was surprised to see one waiting for him that had eluded his notice when it came through. "We're to rendezvous with her at the Nevada Club. It seems she has a private table in the high-rollers lounge."

"Nothing like staying incognito at a busy casino, with cameras every square meter and dozens of security personnel," Milo quipped.

"Rosen probably keeps a close eye on her most of the time. She's the epitome of a loose cannon, I imagine. How do you want to play this?"

"That's more like it! Finally creating a partnership here," he replied with a pseudo-zeal. "She's not wanted on anything I can do anything about, or I don't think she is at least. I'll follow your lead, secret agent man."

Hal gave him a furtive look, but softened when he noticed Milo almost straining himself trying to keep a straight face. "I suppose the whole 'good cop, bad cop' routine might come in handy with her... as long as she's not armed."

"But, wouldn't I have to play both roles then, since I'm the actual cop?"

"She doesn't know that, unless she's exceptionally perceptive."

"Eh, no matter. I prefer the Colombo routine anyway. It tends to disarm people most of the time."

Chapter Eleven: Double Down

Former Petty Officer First Class Raymus Watson stood motionless in the shower within his hotel room at the Atlantis Casino in Reno. He had hoped the cold water would help numb him from the immense guilt he was feeling, but after thirty minutes of being chilled to the bone, he realized it was time to try something else.

In his particular predicament, many might consider staying in a busy hotel and casino to be an amateur move. Watson would tell those people that there are significant differences between hiding and blending in. He was a noted expert at hiding in plain sight, and his dark complexion made it easy for him to alternate between black, Latino, Indian, and Persian with a simple change in garment or grooming.

There was a more strategic reason he chose to stay at the Atlantis however; it was adjacent to the Rosen Network headquarters. He had only been in Reno a few hours, after four transfers on the train to be sure he had lost his pursuers, and he had already tested Rosen's perimeter security. The best money could buy; and as much security as a small country. Lucky for Watson, he had bested security to rival the most impressive of many medium-sized countries.

Accepting the futility of washing away his sins, Watson shut off the water and watched as it rushed past the blue tile and down the chromed drain cover. He dried and dressed as efficiently as if he were still on active duty. Once done, he stood and stared at his empty room. While it had the standard hotel faire: two full beds, single desk and chair, entertainment cabinet, and lounge chair, it depressed Raymus to admit that places such as these were more of a home to him than where his kin still lived since he was a child. He did a quick inspection of the room and was satisfied with what he concluded. To anyone who happened onto the room, it would appear that no one had been there.

When he checked in, he provided two names: Frank Jansen; an alias he'd used only one other time, and Bria Calpamos, who he introduced as a colleague. It's far less suspicious for two people to be traveling together than one, and even less so when they pay with what would appear to be a business account. While physical money was still available, the near universal acceptance of a few forms of crypto currency made hiding and accessing money practically effortless, and safe from prying eyes.

Although quite adept at hacking into mini-bars so he wouldn't be charged, Watson opted to make himself a cocktail with liquor from the room assigned to his phony co-worker, Bria, to keep up the charade. After just a few sips he felt incredibly tired. It had been a long and exhausting day. He checked the time and saw there was still about eight hours until the hunt, so he decided to indulge himself a little with some rest before the next phase of his mission.

Raymus had rarely found hotel beds comfortable, or acceptably hygienic, so he grabbed a pillow and lay down between them, with his arms crossed like a mummy. He doubted he would sleep long, but just in case he set an alarm for four in the morning; giving him one hour to infiltrate Rosen until the game resumed.

Milo's Studebaker landed at the auto valet for the Stateline Resort and Casino on the Nevada side of Lake Tahoe. Milo watched anxiously as the mechanical arms and platforms of the computerized parking system efficiently shelved his car as if it were packaged produce being put into storage. He couldn't recall the last time one of the automated parking systems had failed, resulting in damage to vehicles, but he remained skeptical of the lack of human touch nonetheless.

They walked through a maze of hallways on their way to the club, all of which had different themes from the casino's various incarnations. For just over a hundred years, Harvey's and Harrah's stood as gateway pillars at the border of California and Nevada. Since both casinos were owned by the same company for much of that time, the two properties merged in 2059 to become the Stateline Gateway Resort as a retro way to return to their roots.

The Nevada Club was in one of the underground tunnels connecting the casinos, and also where some of the more private shows took place. Hal and Milo entered the club and were met with dubious stares. They scanned the area but didn't see anyone resembling

Sonya. Fortunately, the maitre'd approached them, and after a few moments of convincing her that they were in the right place, and that Sonya was expecting them, they were led to a quiet corner obscured from the entrance by some astonishing architecture.

They entered the space and were taken aback at how it felt as if they'd stepped into an entirely different area. While still part of the open club, with full visibility of the stage and most of the bar, the room was slightly elevated and noticeably brighter. The furniture was of a higher quality with a more homely feel to them, and there were service call panels within arm's length from every position in the quaint yet cozy den.

"It's plastoid-composite glass under mimetic holographic shadowing," Sonya said, noting their awe. She looked them over for a couple seconds and sized them up thoroughly. "You boys look like you've worn a uniform not too long ago. What are we working with here?"

Milo and Hal traded impressed looks and sat down on the soft, coffee-colored leather settee. "Army, retired," Milo offered. "Ended my service as a TRADOC instructor. Before that, I was 31 Bravo."

Hal paused a moment, considering what and how much he should reveal about himself. Then he remembered that Sonya had served with his wife. Not knowing what Lindsey had shared with her, he decided to be honest but as succinct as Milo had been.

"Navy, corpsman. I was actually with your sister company, the Crazy 88s, for most of Operation Errant Hunt, until you moved on to bigger and better things that is," Hal finished with a derisive glare.

Sonya matched his steely gaze for a brief moment before responding. "Bigger, maybe. Better, definitely not; at least not for a while. You're captain... pardon me, Colonel Dune's husband? I pictured you... I dunno, more like *him* I guess," she rebuked gesturing toward Milo.

Hal redirected his disdain toward his beaming partner, but felt a response was still warranted. "I'm the lucky one in the relationship, no argument from me there."

Following an extended awkward pause, Sonya ordered a drink, and the other two followed suit. Her blood-red Manhattan, and their Sierra Nevada beers, seemed to arrive almost instantly, prompting her to reopen their dialog.

"Sorry for the brush-off boys, but it's been a long time since I've met with someone outside the company, alone anyway."

"No need to be bashful," Milo assured, "this is a chance meeting for us as well. You may find that we have very similar concerns as yours."

"Oh? And what might those concerns be?" She countered, with a defensive edge.

"For starters," Hal cut in after a large swig of his beer, "that you're beginning to wonder how your company is recruiting its contestants. Ones whose skills seem to be getting uncomfortably close to being on par with your own."

She looked wide-eyed at the both of them for several seconds. "How could you *possibly* know that? I haven't mentioned that suspicion to anyone."

"We didn't. You just told us," Milo answered for them both. "But it was a logical conclusion considering you reached out to your former company commander as a means of exploring options you hadn't tried before. Questioning authority can be a healthy thing on occasion, if it's done right and with appropriate intentions."

"Fair enough," she said staring down into her drink as if it held some prophetic message. "So how bad is it? It seems like they keep magically finding criminals who were also part of a special military or law enforcement group." She paused a moment to look up at them. "They *are* criminals, aren't they?"

Milo sat back and stayed quiet. He knew this was Hal's area of expertise. He then reached the nearest call panel and ordered everyone another drink, since he figured there would be plenty of time, and Sonya was likely comped or had an ongoing tab.

"What you might consider 'criminals' is somewhat of a subjective term in this case," Hal began after a large inhale. "But it was hardly magical in how your latest... opponents, for lack of a better term, were chosen. Your employers, and the Department of Corrections, have had an under-the-table partnership for nearly as long as you've been a hunter. I can't say for sure when or how this partnership turned ugly, but there's evidence that your current competitor, Marcus Hyde is his name, and at least the two contestants before him were recruited through fabricated criminal charges. These men were specifically targeted due to their military experience and training."

Hal paused when the second round of drinks arrived, which prompted him to quickly down the remainder of his first as if someone were going to take it away from him. Sonya didn't seem to notice, continuing to hold her crystal tumbler with slowly diluting spirits. Hal opened his mouth to continue his tirade when she spoke up first.

"So prisoner 74... I mean Hyde, has false charges? I was told he's been accused of rape. And the guy before him, the one they called Jean, he was part of a prescription drug scheme."

Hal saw that Sonya was becoming very uneasy. Although it pained him as a doctor, he conceded that a little discomfort on her part was the least of his concerns right now. "As I suspect was the intention, those were half-truths, and I'd wager there have been more. Marcus was accused of *statutory* rape, of the consenting 17-year-old daughter of a prominent Air Force General. While that doesn't make him innocent per se, it certainly doesn't mean he deserves to go to Leavenworth, or to be forced into participating in your blood-sport. All before he sees some semblance of due process I might add. He was actually in our custody barely twelve hours ago, until Rosen goons took him away like someone reclaiming property that was stolen."

Sonya was as still as a statue for a long moment. Suddenly, she gulped the rest of the drink she held in her hand, then took a large swig of the second. She sat back in a slouch, as if trying to hide in the soft, dark cushions. Hal was expecting a response from her, but when none came he resumed.

"Julius Archer, the man referred to as Jean, was actually arrested for attempting to purchase cheaper medication for his sick wife, from an illegal source, due to their insurance not covering some of the care of her illness. Again, not technically innocent, but I think we can agree that that's hardly death penalty territory. Now, it seems pretty clear that this situation doesn't sit well with you. I don't know what *real* authority you have with Rosen, but I'd wager it's more than you might think."

Another awkward pause. The two agents took a few more drinks of their beer, in between expectant stares at Sonya, but they waited for her to respond. The background music began to fade and Milo turned to see a lone guitarist take the stage.

"So," she finally blurted out after several minutes, "you think I have more authority than none? How does that work? I know full well that I'm little more than a commodity. I'm on ice so thin that if I move I get wet."

"I can't say I'm a fan of what you do," Milo interjected, ignoring the looks from the others who appeared to forget he was there, "or know much about it either. But don't you always tag in during the third bout?"

"As the Chief Hunter, yes I do… Usually. What are you suggesting? That I somehow throw the match? Assuming he even *makes it* past the second hunter?"

"In a manner of speaking, yes. There are a number of ways to do that: non-lethal rounds, finding a way to communicate with him covertly, appearing to be bested by him, et cetera. Judging by my few minutes with him and viewing his first match, I don't believe he'll kill you unless he has no choice."

Sonya slinked lower in her seat. She was far from the collected, confident person Hal and Milo saw on the Network, on the rare occasions they watched her. Her current composure resembled that of someone backed into a corner with no way out.

"One last thing," Hal offered. "We were actually sent to locate, and re-integrate, three escaped fugitives who were also targeted by Rosen. Marcus Hyde is one of them. They were all part of special operations in their respective branches of service. They also all share one significant experience with you."

She slowly looked up at him, and didn't turn away as she worked out what he was getting at. "My implant?"

"Your ASI, yes," he confirmed as they all finished their drinks simultaneously. She knew then what she was up against, and they began to brainstorm options on how to proceed.

Chapter Twelve: Round 2

Milo and Hal departed the Stateline Club and headed toward Reno. Sonya pledged to contact them if she learned anything helpful, but asked them to lay low to avoid arousing suspicion and await her signal, unless there was some sort of emergency. Due to its proximity to the Network's headquarters, she recommended they stay at the Atlantis Resort. Hal was attempting to book a couple of rooms, as close together as possible, while Milo smoothly piloted his Stude out of the auto parking garage.

"Refresh my memory," Milo interjected, breaking the silence that ensued after they were airborne. "What are ASIs again?"

"Advanced Synaptic Implants," Hal answered without looking up from his tablet. "Most covert operatives and spec ops personnel are given one now, after their apparent uncontested success on service members during the war."

"Given? You mean they have a choice about it?"

"Actually yes. It's completely voluntary, if you qualify for it that is. Screening happens *after* acceptance into special teams, and since that process is arduous enough as it is, around 75% are offered one following return from their first successful mission."

"What is it supposed to do? I've heard of them before but never knew their actual purpose. Seems like it would break Geneva Convention rules, or something."

"That's because, even after more than ten years, they're still SCI-level clearance. From what I've been told -- not by doctors or experts mind you -- is that it *enhances* everything. Speed, agility, strength. Even higher brain functions to support strategy for tactical situations. Did you read any of the articles on Ghost Squad; the team Sonya was part of for a time during the war?"

"Of course. Hard not to once the rumors started to come out a few years after the armistice. That's the sort of thing legends are made of."

"Well, I can tell you that all, or at least most, of what you read is true. Their squad members survived behind enemy lines for over three weeks with only enough food, water, and ammo to last one. Some of that was due to training, which I'm sure I don't have to mention to you," Hal remarked wryly as he looked over at the former Army instructor. "That team was a test-bed for the ASIs in combat however. Not one of its members claimed they were ever tired, anxious, hungry, or unprepared for... *anything*. Granted, some of their testimony could be chalked up to machoism and the like, but official reports claimed they were ordered to be truthful and cooperative. Also, while there are several methodologies to gaining stronger conscious control over one's body, the ASI is designed to focus only essential functions like a laser beam to survival and adaptation."

"So, this implant turns people into machines? Seems like there would be a lot of downsides to that, or at least there ought to be."

"There are, or *were* anyway, unofficial reports alleging that around twenty percent had problems adjusting to the implants. Side effects ranging from acute mania to catatonia were noted. The agency I work for has been looking for these individuals to interview for years; a single one has yet to be located. Then there are the ones who simply can't turn off or ignore the heightened senses from their implants…"

After a full minute awkward pause, Milo considered letting the man alone with his thoughts. Alternatively though, "I'm sorry, were you going to follow up on that last comment?" Hal looked at him like he didn't know what he was talking about, so Milo continued. "*Twenty* percent!? That's considered acceptable losses for some of the best trained men and women this country's military has to offer? Just so they *might* become better at their jobs in the heat of battle? That is downright appalling! Particularly for an all-volunteer military force since 1973. People don't sign up for that crap anymore!"

Hal's face contorted into a mien of offense. "Why does it sound like you're blaming *me* for this? I've had zero involvement in this whole operation until I was recruited to find evidence against the use of ASIs two years ago!"

"Whoa, hold on a minute. Calm down. I'm not blaming anybody. I'm just angry is all. The deeper I get into this rabbit hole, the more pissed I get about finding some justice for war heroes. It's a weakness of mine. But let's not forget we have one more fugitive out there to find. Watson isn't just going to come up to us wearing a name tag."

"Maybe it will be that simple. He's directly involved with Rosen and the prison break. That's at least one thing I'm confident of. His level of immersion still remains a mystery though. I'm sure our paths will cross sooner rather than later."

~

Raymus Watson readjusted his chameleon jacket for a third time, while walking out the main entrance of the Atlantis as casually as he could. Though it was nearly five in the morning, he wasn't the only person coming and going at that hour. Lonely spinsters ending a long night of gambling. Wait staff coming to relieve their cohorts from the unenviable graveyard shift. Early risers emerging from their rooms to be the first to enjoy the cornucopia of breakfast buffets. A casino was an indefatigable organism, with strange but regular patterns that one could jump into at any time throughout the year.

It took Watson longer to clear the expansive casino property than he anticipated, but once he did he activated one of the preset programs of his jacket. The concealed, optical fibers imbedded within the fabric began to change color and texture, like a ripple on a tranquil pond. In seconds, the unassuming grey jacket bore a striking resemblance to the navy blue coats worn by Rosen Security, right down to the neon green logo patch and matching elbow pads.

Given the razor-thin timetable, Raymus was unable to procure the security team's current comlink apparatus. Instead, he obtained the previous model used by the company and installed a bandwidth enhancer. He was confident that were he discovered, no one could tell the difference, even under strict scrutiny.

The final test to gain access into the building would be the ID card. He didn't have the time or equipment to duplicate the intricately complex device, so he lifted one from a hapless employee of similar-enough build and complexion who had just finished his shift during Watson's earlier excursion to the exclusive campus. He quickly discovered that the card works in concert with its assigned owner's imbedded personal data chip, so both have to be synced to allow access around the network's properties. He just hoped the equipment he *did* have was sensitive enough to link the frequency of the employee it belonged to.

Raymus was mentally preparing to introduce himself under his new guise, Louis Salvatoré, as he approached the first checkpoint. There was no physical security at the outer door, just a multi-phasic reader inside a mirrored alcove. Once a scan of the ID card, imbedded chip, and several body-type comparisons was completed, the door opened to a second checkpoint where two security officers were posted 24/7.

"Has it started yet?" Watson asked, referring to the next round of Most Dangerous Game, while his stolen, altered ident combo was being inspected. One of the security officers slowly looked up with tired eyes to regard him, then back down to a hidden display under the desk.

"Any minute now. What you doing back Louis? Your shift ended hours ago."

"I have a sit-down with Lujayne. Thought it'd be easier than messaging her. Figured she'd still want me in uniform." Rhea Lujayne was the Security Director. Raymus gambled that her position was high enough the average grunt wouldn't know or have access to her schedule. But not someone so outlandish as to arise suspicion.

The elder, more senior officer finally became interested. "I didn't know that was an option. I've been here four years, and I've never talked to her one-on-one. Do me a favor will ya, and let her know that?"

Years of tradecraft in espionage still didn't prepare even the most skilled spy to remain completely calm when you think your cover has been blown. Watson had prepared for infiltration missions with limited time and resources many times in the past, but never on US soil, without support of *any* kind. And especially not when there were lives at stake that he had personally put in harm's way through a lapse in judgement a rookie could've discerned.

"Sure thing, if I get the chance," he answered with a nervous smile. "I've never talked to her before either. Gotta first get a sense of the landscape before moving off course though; know what I mean?"

The other two nodded in unison and went back to whatever held their attention before he arrived. Raymus made his way down the short hallway and waited for the lift. He let out his breath the instant the lift doors closed in front of him, easing some of his tension along with it. He took a moment to memorize the building directory that was displayed on a glowing panel, and opted for the seventh floor. Lucky for him, Lujayne's office was on the same floor as his true destination; Rosen's records division.

The lift stopped and doors parted to reveal a sobering bright waiting area. He pulled his cap lower, to further shield his eyes. From that angle, he could clearly see his reflection in the glossy black floor. Looking around for an indicator of where to go, Watson got the sense that the seventh floor was rarely occupied by anyone other than those who had offices there.

There were two plush, cream-colored leather form-chairs at opposing ends of the foyer. They looked as if they had never been used. He approached the one on his left, to further support his theory, when a holographic banner appeared in the hallway. In bold, red lettering it read 'Rhea Lujayne, Security Director' equal distance from floor to ceiling. He backed up two paces and the banner faded away as casually as it appeared.

There was only one other route to take, so he turned around and confidently walked through the bright blue simulacrum of the records division. He turned a corner and was met by a short hallway with two doors; one to a unisex lavatory, and the other was a magnetically sealed transparent slider with a lone card reader. On the other side was a single work station sandwiched between large digital archives. He waved the appropriated ID card over the scanner and the door silently slid aside, allowing him entry into the claustrophobic chamber.

Raymus sat on the stiffly uncomfortable chair and placed his data stick into the reader. The display came to life and asked for a username. Before he began to try some of the names he committed to memory, he thought it best to try to bypass the system by attempting a general word or phrase ubiquitous to computer systems. His first instinct was to type Guest, due to a silly inside joke with his former colleagues over mutual appreciation of an older television show. He laughed out loud when access was granted past the logon.

The man wearing a nametag that read L. Salvatoré looked on patiently as his data stick came to life and began searching for its pre-programmed targets: all network contestants of the past two years who are veterans, and where they had been referred from. While that list compiled, which Watson predicted to take only a minute at most, he did a search for close associations of the company based on frequency of communication, as well as any major donors and stakeholders.

The universal reader light turned green, indicating completion of its download, but Raymus continued to peruse the list of names and companies that Rosen held in regard. The list contained the usual wealthy investors, low-profile politicians, government contracts, and commercial financiers. Two names however stood out amongst the barrage of funders: the Alethea Foundation and the National Institute of Mental Health. He saved the content of his additional search results to his data stick and checked the time. He had only been there three minutes thus far, and had no intention of staying longer than five. So his last order of business was to look for any active or recent clandestine operations, and who may be carrying them out.

Suddenly, the peaceful hum of processors in that small space was pierced by a shift from the calming blue light to hellish red, and an angry automated announcement blasting into every corner of the building, he assumed, instantly followed.

"Attention all personnel. Priority one programming will commence in thirty minutes. Report to your designated areas within department accepted time-frames. Thank you for your dedication to this neighborhood network."

Watson ensured his downloads had concluded and casually left the confining records room. He turned the corner to see a strikingly tall and imposing woman waiting for the lift. He quickly recalled that there was only one other office on the floor, and soon recognized Lujayne from the bio he read prior to embarking on his mission. Her stature still gave him pause nonetheless.

"Ma'am," he said with a tilt of his head. She gave him a curt nod in response, then did a double take.

"What were you doing over there officer...?"

"Salvatoré ma'am. I'm actually off shift. I seem to have misplaced a memento from the company store for my partner and I'm retracing my steps to see if I can locate it. I haven't been having much luck with that."

"I see," she responded with skepticism. Her speech pattern had a strange staccato style to it, and undertones of her Haitian accent still remained.

The lift doors opened and he deferred to her to enter first. Two long strides and she cleared the length of the lift car. He entered not knowing which direction they were headed. She selected floor 13, while he reluctantly chose the ground floor. The instant the doors closed she squared off with him and loomed like she were about to squash a bug. Watson didn't dare look her in the eye for fear of capture.

"I'm putting you on notice officer," she growled, peppering him with spittle. "Prepare for a formal reprimand from your supervisor. Your cap is far too low, your boots look like they haven't been shined since they came out of the box, and your jacket is *not* standard issue. Square yourself away, A-SAP!" The lift doors parted and she stormed out like an incensed giant without looking back.

Raymus rode the lift in silence as others entered and exited on their way to their duty stations. He reached the ground floor without further incident, but walked briskly to the exit where he could see the waxing sunlight beyond the security doors. He was nearly to the door when he froze by a raised voice from his left.

"Hey! How'd it go up there Salvatoré?"

Watson turned slowly to regard the middle-aged security officer whom he chatted with earlier. "Eh, she gave me the runaround. Told me to talk to my supervisor instead. Sorry pal."

"Figures," he muttered cynically. "Thanks for trying though."

Ramus nodded respectfully and hurried out the door, before he overstayed his welcome. His hat was still pulled low, so the bright sunrise directly in front of him didn't require him to shield his eyes. He quickened his pace even more. When he felt he was a comfortable distance away, he activated his jacket's camouflage feature once again by depressing a button inside his cuff, and the garment shifted to a metallic aqua blue, the color of the concierge staff at the Atlantis.

Encouraged by his successful infiltration of Rosen, Watson considered advancing his next move ahead of schedule. He needed to upload his findings to a contact he'd maintained throughout the entire ordeal with Rosen, but he preferred to review the data more thoroughly himself first, and crosscheck it on a DOD ComNet-accessible computer terminal. It was doubtful there would be one at a casino, he concluded, so that left him with few options in downtown Reno. There were a couple military facilities in the region he could easily access, but their distance and the time it would take to prep for such an undertaking wouldn't balance a risk/benefit analysis enough to his liking.

By the time he arrived back at his hotel room, he had settled on one of the last public places with both access to more secure networks, and privacy for those who wished to conduct business in relative safety outside of one's own home; the library. He knew there was one just over the river to the south of where he stood. He thought back to his days in the Boy Scouts, and remembered their motto to be prepared, which brought a wan smile to his face as he sat down to map out step-by-step how he would get there and back without being recognized and captured, or worse.

Chapter Thirteen: Lucky Charm

Hal rubbed his eyes a fourth time since leaving his hotel room. He also bumped into the coffee bar patron in line in front of him while doing so. The stocky, middle-aged balding man wearing a Hawaiian shirt either didn't care or didn't notice. His eyes were so red at that moment, Hal imagined they were glowing and had frightened off any rebuke he might have otherwise received. He conceded that three hours sleep just didn't cut it for him anymore, as he stepped up to the vendor.

He ordered a Gibraltar, with an extra shot of espresso, and a turkey sausage quiche. He weaved his way to the rear of the service area to doctor up his drink when he saw an annoyingly familiar sight. Milo was sitting at a corner table reading peacefully, and looking remarkably well-rested. He also appeared to be wearing a fresh change of clothes, which caused Hal to stand gawkily near the cream and sugar trying to remember if Milo had an overnight bag, while people walked around him sending concerned glares his direction.

"This seat taken?" Hal asked sleepily, as he sat down without waiting for a response. Once he was down however, it crossed his mind to at least check to see if he sat at the right table.

Milo looked up from the scrolling data on the table's built-in monitor. "I'm afraid it was, but it appears that person may have been taken by body snatchers since I last saw him," he bantered. "You up all night gambling or something?"

Hal fitfully stirred his drink and took a large gulp of the still hot beverage, not caring how much it burned his throat. "Not my scene. I reported in, said goodnight to the wife and kid, then collapsed on the bed. Just didn't get enough shut-eye I suppose. I've had sleep issues since we came back from the Far East." He emptied the rest of his coffee and considered getting another. He eventually looked up at Milo to receive an amused stare from the man. "What's got you so chipper this morning? I *know* you didn't get a full night's sleep any more than I did," he jabbed jealously.

Milo's grin turned full smile, and he unfolded his arms. "For me, it's about quality not quantity. While I love sharing a bed with my wife, I've always slept better on my own. The second my head hit the pillow I was out. Didn't even bother to set an alarm."

Hal scoffed and bent over to access the tabletop's screen menu. The display split to accommodate a new user, but kept whatever Milo had been reading unabated. Hal ordered a blended iced mocha for his second round of caffeine, in hopes that the chill would further aid in waking him up. Once the order was complete, the table's screen returned to full size and remained facing Milo. The man no longer seemed interested in what Hal could now comprehend as a news ticker however.

"If you don't mind my saying," Milo posed, "the world of espionage doesn't seem to agree with you. I'm not so sure the illustrious people at DIA are directing you to your full potential... An appropriate use of your time as an MD I mean. They should consider more objectives comparable to your short-lived career at Omnium."

Hal stared at him with a glazed-over look; his head propped up by his arm. He was taking an uncomfortable amount of time to respond, but if asked he would claim it was due to not knowing how much he was able to reveal. The caffeine was beginning to seep into his system, giving him somewhat more clarity, and he didn't see any harm in providing some context to the very logical question.

"Well," he groaned. "This wasn't my initial assignment. I *was* following the earliest recorded test group for the ASIs; a small division of the National Institute of Mental Health, contracted with the Alethea Foundation. That, I can confidently say, was a more suitable fit. Now I find myself trying to juggle *two* operations," he said wearily.

"So what happened to the other team assigned to watch Rosen? Something tells me there's no shortage of fed finks with practically unlimited resources."

"Says the guy driving a Studebaker," Hal rejoined with a solemn tone. He finally felt the fog lifting from his hazy head. "The dynamic team of one went MIA almost two weeks ago. Since I was on a parallel assignment, of sorts, I was re-tasked with finding out what happened to her. I was getting close to her trail when the prison break happened. That's part of the reason why I was at Leavenworth before you," he added after a moment. "I was looking for her, not tipped off for any escape plots."

Milo shrugged. "Makes sense. Any new leads on her whereabouts? Maybe I can help, if you're allowed to give me any details that is."

"Yes and no... regarding new leads. Her name is Alena Sarne, and she was a senior member with the National Institute of Corrections. I don't have all the particulars, but from what I understand, since she was a lieutenant with Naval Intelligence before her current stint, DIA reached out to her to see if she would keep an eye on Rosen's partnership with BOP."

"What, no fancy alias, or compelling cover story like you got?" Milo asked satirically.

"Sorry to disappoint you," Hal fired back as he sucked down the remaining pockets of his blended beverage. The chill was both invigorating to his tired body, and soothing to his scorched throat. "She's legit, so she didn't need one. Plus, from what I hear, she spearheaded a couple of excellent programs for vets who are in custody at federal institutions... which is unrelated to Rosen so I don't know why I felt the need to share that with you."

Milo nodded in thought. His hand came very close to his chin before he stopped himself. "Well, if you'll allow it, I can put an alert out for her as a person of interest. She's one of ours; in more ways than one. It's doubtful to get much pushback trying to find a missing DOJ employee."

"What would putting out an alert entail?" Hal asked askance.

"It would simply put more eyes on her, figuratively speaking. Facial recognition, financial account and social media activity, conspicuous searches... movement of any kind sends a notice to the requesting party, i.e. me."

"And these alerts are fairly common? Setting one up won't raise any eyebrows?"

"In the time it took to explain what one is, a hundred of them probably went active. So no, it's not too likely to be noticed. And even if it were, so what? What harm could it do to put a little attention on her disappearance?"

"For starters, I don't want people grilling you on where you got her name and employer from. I'd rather not put you in a tricky situation if I don't have to, and further endanger her in the process. Assuming that's even a concern at this point."

"Let me worry about my own comfort level, thank you. But I'm not gonna just sit back and…"

Hal's journey back into coherence took a large leap forward when he noticed Milo sit up straighter and stare intently at something, or someone, off to his right. Hal looked around to place what the man might be tracking, but he quickly gave up and decided to ask.

"What? What is it? You look like a lion just spotting his second breakfast."

"I'm pretty sure I just saw Watson. He exited that lift bank over there and is heading toward the direction of the south exit."

Hal began haphazardly scanning the area. "You're joking. I don't see him. What would he be doing here anyway?"

Milo stood and waved his right hand over the table, settling the bill and resetting the imbedded display. He tapped a spot a few centimeters behind his left ear and gave Hal an impatient glare.

"I don't know, let's go ask him. Does your subdermal communicator still work?"

Hal leapt up and fell in beside him. "Yes. In fact it's been upgraded and linked with my imbedded mobile. What channel you on?"

"Three," Milo answered his pace quickening. "I doubt we'll be able to cut him off, but you flank him on the left in case he tries to double back. I'll head the direction I last saw him and meet you on the other side of this gaming island. He was wearing a grey jacket and a Vegas Knights ball cap."

Hal nodded and the pair went their separate ways. The relentless drone of strobing lights from gaming machines attracted people of various ages like moth to flame. He waded through the endless twilight, dodging half-intoxicated gamblers as they buzzed from one game to the next. Hal had never been fond of casinos, or gambling in general. They often brought in some very appealing shows and exhibits, he reflected, but he found the experience not worth the sensory overload casinos imposed upon their patrons.

He turned the corner to another long aisle of electronic games bookending the path, with some tables farther down the walkway. Milo appeared in front of him about a third of the way down his field of vision. He briefly turned around to heed any goings-on in Hal's direction, then continued his alleged pursuit. He had forgotten about the subdermal communicator being online, and upon hearing Milo's voice, nearly jumped out of his shoes.

"Anything?" Milo asked, his voice sounding as clear as if he were standing directly beside him.

"All clear on my end. Do you see him up ahead?"

"I think he's just passing that sports bar at the bend. I'm gonna pick up the pace a bit, as discreetly as I can so he doesn't suspect I'm tracking him."

He thinks, Hal repeated in his head. "Copy. I'll do the same." Hal threw any discretion to the wind and began to jog. He didn't doubt his partner's perceptiveness, but having not seen Watson himself, it proved difficult to track the man with the same level of zeal.

~

Raymus Watson wasted no time upon returning from Rosen. He checked out of the room under his assumed name, via the in-room concierge system, but kept the room assigned to Bria, so it seemed at least one person stayed to enjoy the local festivities a bit. He was casually dressed and sporting some hockey gear, since the season had just begun a couple weeks prior.

He was making his way to the south exit when he sensed he was being followed. Even during his time as a SEAL, Watson had the uncanny ability of knowing when he was being watched. He didn't know if that was an effect of his ASI, or something he had before he volunteered for that grand experiment. One thing he was sure of however, memories of his life *before* the implant are now irrevocably blurred.

Raymus passed a sports lounge on his right at a bend in the walkway. The next round of the Most Dangerous Game would be starting any minute, so he entered the establishment and asked the barista to switch on Rosen in an attempt to draw in a crowd. He didn't linger to see if it worked, since it was still relatively early in the morning, but he did activate his chameleon jacket once again to change it from grey to a golden brown.

As Watson approached the doors to the exit, he slowed a moment to peer into the highly reflective glass. The sports fans were growing at a trickle. Out of the ambling customers, he spotted two men that didn't quite fit in with the crowd. One was tall, approaching middle-age, and had a haircut so obviously military that the man might as well have been in uniform. The other, who had just managed to catch up with the first, seemed more aloof, but was clearly a G-man based on his attire and general amateurish technique of pursuit.

The soldier paused to scan the sports café, very thoroughly. He quickly determined that his quarry wasn't inside and looked directly at him, in the same moment the doors leading outside parted. Raymus knew he had to disappear, and in a way he wouldn't normally choose; for many reasons. He hailed a Johnny Cab, and directed it to go to the Nevada Museum of Art, since it was close to the library. The robotic head and torso acknowledged the request, in its annoyingly chipper voice, and even tipped its hat before turning and speeding away. He glanced toward the doors of the south exit for as long as it was in his line of sight, but his pursuers were nowhere to be seen. He let out a sigh of relief, but as quietly as he could so to not alert the robot driver.

While there were a number of reasons he was adverse to the Johnson Cab Company fleet, his primary objections were twofold: it was relatively easy to track when used, and by whom. Then there was the fact that they just plain creeped him out. It was like the things were straight out of a campy movie from the 1990s.

Traffic was lighter than expected in the early weekday hours, so he calculated arriving at the museum in less than fifteen minutes. His so-called 'driver' reminded him that his destination didn't open until ten o'clock. He thanked him for the information to prevent additional reminders. Downtown Reno not being as picturesque to look at as many other major cities, Raymus instead contemplated which of the data he downloaded to share with his new handler, for lack of a better term.

When she first contacted him, it had seemed both highly suspicious, and desperately providential. She sent an encrypted message on one of the old ComNet channels he still sparingly used. It was even an encryption method commonly used by Naval Intelligence, so he was intimately familiar with the sequence.

The first message came mere minutes after his meeting with Rosen recruiters, while he was on assignment in Belarus no less. He had to admit, the offer from Rosen's representatives to head their asset procurement division was a tempting one, but he got the sense that they weren't giving him the full picture. He told the reps that he would give them an answer once his mission was completed, and they parted ways amicably. Before he had time to think about it however, he heard a chime indicating receipt of a message on a channel he hadn't used in years:

"Ur about to be made. They don't take kindly to rejection. How do you suppose they found you while in the field?"

That question had occurred to him as well, so he had made sure to ask the pair sent to recruit him. Their answer was that 'they had friends in high places,' or some such redirect. He later learned that they had been accurate, from a certain point of view. As he watched rival agents raid the room he had just occupied, from a vacant apartment across the street, he received another message from his guardian angel claiming an analyst had sold him out, rather than be blackmailed. Raymus was fairly confident he knew who that was referring to, and would deal with him the first chance he could, but before he sought to find a safe extraction point, he replied to the mysterious messenger: 'who is this, and what do you want?'

"For now, you can call me your Lucky Charm," came the cryptic response.

~

Alena Sarne was feeling trapped. Out of all the large hotels in Reno, it was amazingly hapless to pick the one that both Watson and the federal agents were staying in as well; though in retrospect it made sense considering its proximity to Rosen. She came down to the coffee bar and froze when she noticed the taller of the two already there and reading from his table's computer. It took her a few seconds, and comments from impatient people, to realize that she and him had never met, and that he would have no reason to be looking for her.

She picked a seat on the opposite side of the food court-like area so she could keep an eye on him. Sitting and tenuously enjoying her coffee and a fresh pastry, she ran scenarios through her head to try and make sense of how the agents would've been led to Rosen's doorstep. No average grunt within the US Marshals could know about the conspiracy between the Network and Department of Corrections, amongst others. Only one possibility remained; these two were getting outside information. From who or where remained to be seen, but her current situation didn't enable her to find out.

The shorter of the dynamic duo arrived and looked like hell. He seemed surprised to see the other one, but brusquely plopped down across from the man anyway. They got to chatting about something fairly in depth, so she allowed her adrenaline level to drop a little once again. She finished her pastry and was sipping her coffee when she looked up to see the bigger one staring in her direction, with a shocked look of recognition in his eyes. The other one was scanning the area haphazardly, but she could feel her heart rate rising back up, freezing her in place again.

They got up and were weaving their way as directly toward her as the dispersion of café style tables allowed them. Panic began to settle upon her, and all she could do in response was to bury her head and appear as if she were engrossed in something displayed on her table monitor. There were still so many things that had to be done, and she knew they would fall through the cracks if she were taken into custody, particularly concerning Watson. While he was more than capable on his own, she put him on his current path and would be devastated if she weren't allowed to follow through with it.

The two were now at her table, the taller one almost completely overshadowing the other from her seated perspective. She tried to calm herself by thinking about what she was going to say, when she looked up to see they had passed her by at a quick pace. They had split up, presumably in search of someone else, and soon disappeared into the hive of gambling machinery.

The level of relief she felt was palpable. So much so that she nearly teared up out of the sheer joy of being able to finish what she had started. Which brought her to the next problem she needed to solve; how was Watson going to send out the data he retrieved? Certainly not through the regular internet, she reckoned. One of the few viable options to upload sensitive data securely was through the ComNet, which was monitored with less scrutiny since anyone with access had, or still has, significant military experience. Figuring out where he would attempt to logon would be where their official meeting place will be.

Chapter Fourteen: Carpe Furor

Milo stood at the ride-share post of the Atlantis's south exit, and continued his visual sweep of the area. Hal stood beside him with a self-satisfied look about him. "Want to re-evaluate that whole quality versus quantity thing again?" Hal razzed.

"What the hell is that supposed to mean; I *saw* him I tell you!" Milo answered incensed. "He must have one of those chameleon jackets; it changed colors when he stepped into the sports café."

Hal could tell he had struck a nerve, so he thought it best to change the subject. "Speaking of that, it looked like the Game was about to start. Where were we going to meet with Kane again?"

"We weren't *meeting* with her anywhere. She was supposed to contact us when she found us a way in to interview one of Rosen's higher-ups," Milo answered in a huff, still scanning the vicinity. "She said the best time would be during the second round, since everyone involved with the production would be otherwise occupied."

"Oh right," Hal mumbled, trying his best to play dumb. "It might be a good idea to poke around there anyway and test their hospitality. Plus we can be close by when Sonya messages. We should probably check in on Marcus before we head over there though. I can empty the tank at that café while we're at it."

Milo grunted and they went back inside. The sport-themed establishment was festively decorated with memorabilia from several different eras of professional and collegiate athletics. These eras were separated into rooms throughout the eatery, which apparently catered to conventional dining habits by making itself a coffee bar in the mornings, then shifting to the more traditional type of bar later on.

The Most Dangerous Game had indeed begun, and could be viewed anywhere one sat or stood. It wouldn't have surprised Milo to find at least one monitor in the lavatories either, a hunch Hal was about to find out for himself as he headed that way.

Milo sat at a tall table in the relatively vacant soccer and hockey room. The seating area wasn't chosen because he considered himself a fan of the two sports, nor was it due to its lower occupancy at the moment. No, in the few seconds he stood in the doorway, Milo instinctively looked for the place that could view all the exits and as much of the café as possible. This was a habit most veterans who have had any combat training continue long after they separate from service.

By the look of what was on the numerous screens and holographic projectors, there was a recap of the first round streaming across the entire restaurant. Even though it was still fresh in Milo's mind, watching Hyde defeat McCone with pure guile was an impressive sight to behold. Although he still felt a twinge of guilt for not fighting to keep the man in his custody a little harder, there was a certain level of satisfaction in how Hyde dispatched the experienced policeman and hunter. He tried to convince himself that he could react with equal cunning in a similar situation, but he was having difficulty believing it.

Almost as if Rosen read his mind from across the street, the broadcast changed to introduce the next hunter chosen for the second round, which caused the pride he was feeling to wane markedly. Five minutes into the program the night before was the most he'd ever watched of the Game, but he somehow knew the selected hunter wasn't announced beforehand in the first round only. Nevertheless, it came as a shock to him when he realized the man being introduced by lead announcer Joram Bachman was known to him. Milo would occasionally be asked to provide remedial courses on the importance of chain-of-command to those who had disobeyed orders one too many times, for domestic and foreign soldiers alike. The face on full display around the room was one of those students, before he found his niche and didn't have to worry about taking orders much anymore.

"While his real name is of course Jack Ridton," Bachman announced in his incessant rant-style of speaking, "he's known to most around here as Wraith because of his seamless way of blending into his environment, and striking completely without warning. He can make himself look like literally *anything*. One of our intrepid contestants could be leaning against a rock wall, or so he thinks. As everyone watching relaxes in a moment of respite, the rock comes to life, and strikes with the precision of a surgeon... if a surgeon had any inclination to actually doing harm that is," he joked.

That pronouncement motivated the handful or so present to cheer loud enough to equate the noise of a crowd twice its size. The slow trickle of bystanders into the café was also increasing due to the enthused shouting. Milo's confidence in Hyde continued to dip however, when he saw the so-called hunting grounds for the next match. Marcus would now be out in the open, and going up against a foe he had neither trained for nor had experience against, as far as Milo's comprehension of the training regimen of Colonial Cavalry went anyway.

Once again, as if the show's producers had a direct link to his mind, another reveal made his apprehension for Hyde's victory continue to descend.

"Another well-known... idiosyncrasy shall we say, about Wraith," Bachman continued, "is that he likes to switch up his weapon of choice. To stay fresh in a variety of tools of the trade, as it were. For this hunt, Wraith has decided to arm himself with an auto-bow; a fascinating fusion of an antique crossbow with modern reloading and targeting technology. While it may not be as crowd-pleasing as the flamethrower he used during his last match, or as unique as the pair of black powder musket-style pistols from last year, Wraith always seems to find ways of livening up the match. So without further adieu, the Game is afoot!"

The displayed image drastically changed to what looked like a satellite view of North America. There was another shift to show the sun peeking over the horizon, near where the International Dateline sat Milo assumed, to signify a new day. Then, as if to project the sensation of casually falling from the heavens, multiple cameras seamlessly zoomed in to a vast expanse of eastern Nevada. In a mesmerizing, awe-inspired display of live camera feeds, the trek from space to Zone Jupiter finally landed to show a serene Marcus Hyde carefully preparing a field ration kit as if it were a gourmet meal. Despite the depressingly dire situation, Milo couldn't help but smile at the young man as he continued to amaze.

Milo's grin must've been much larger than intended, because it stopped Hal dead in his tracks upon returning from the fresher. Hal looked around with heavy suspicion for several seconds until landing on one of the many holoprojections, instantly becoming equally impressed.

"Is he doctoring up a K-Ration?"

"Looks like," Milo answered reverently.

"Damn, that sure takes me back. Some of my best meals to this day came from one of those little bricks... well, most *memorable* anyway."

Hyde looked to be just finishing his peaceful meal when he was startled by a short, booming noise. The sound was similar to that of a cannon firing, indicating the start of a new round with the arrival of a hunter. Hal noticed the immediate change in his demeanor, which transitioned from a sobering contentedness to one of focused determination.

Marcus quickly, yet meticulously, packed what little gear he had lying about and moved at a fast clip in the opposite direction of the noise made by the landing craft. While he knew the craft carried someone there to kill him, he was completely oblivious to who it was and what skills he or she may be carrying with them; exactly the same as with the previous hunter wearing the World War II-era jacket and helmet.

Like most soldiers, sailors, marines, and airmen who received specialized training, his instincts had taken over and it had all come down to who had the sharper mind on their feet. Marcus would've been perfectly gratified with surviving the designated twelve hours, or making it to one of the two safety rings within each zone, the only two other ways to end a match, but he saw an opportunity to significantly delay his opponent and took to it with no regrets... or at least none that would've made him proceed differently if given the chance.

The camera angle changed to show a man casually descending the ramp of a landing craft, wearing a highly sophisticated, adaptive ghillie suit. Even with the simple task of stepping into the dirt and rock that made up the natural environment of Zone Jupiter's outside arena, the suit's bio-matrix composite material modified itself to meet its new surroundings in a ripple-like effect. As the craft departed, the hooded figure surveyed the quiet area; a perfectly balanced region of sand, greenery and rock formations. Now alone, standing in front of the recently vacated landing pad, he peeled back his cowl to reveal a man so unkempt it looked like he had just fought a bear in a stream after years of living in the woods.

Despite his lack of any semblance of grooming standards, Ridton still received some random cheers from the morning audience faire. Milo, on the other hand, audibly scoffed at the holographically-projected image, which prompted a chuckle from Hal seated adjacent to him.

The hunter referred to as Wraith bent to one knee; the auto-bow slung tightly to his back moving ever so slightly. From pouches sewn into his flanks, he pulled two pairs of miniature seeker drones and released them to search out his prey. As the spherical devices buzzed away like angry bees, in all different directions, he freed the auto-bow from its sling on his back and began to walk toward one of the drones' pre-determined flight paths. Milo wasn't the least bit surprised by that cocksure attitude, and was genuinely hoping he had chosen the wrong drone to follow.

Projections and screens around the café split into three views: Marcus fleeing from a seemingly nearby Wraith at a composed pace, bisected by an animated Bachman unnecessarily describing what everyone watching had just witnessed, adding his predictions of what was to come. The scene was visually grating. Milo and Hal looked to each other and rolled their eyes.

"This could go on for hours before they even catch a glimpse of one another," Milo said optimistically. Hal mumbled his concurrence as he turned back to the nearest screen. Almost on cue, Milo's smart watch alerted him to a priority message, which prompted a dubious look from Hal.

"That's funny," Milo announced, contorting his brow slightly in thought. "We got a potential hit on your wayward contact from NIC. Seventy-three percent match for one Alena Sarne. Right here in Reno no less. That can't be a coincidence."

"What!?" Hal interjected, practically falling out of his chair. "When did you send out her alert? I hadn't received approval for you to do that yet!"

Milo leaned back and folded his arms; a satisfied smirk broaching his neutral façade. "While we were walking back from the carport, after losing Watson... I *did* see him by the way, even if *you* didn't."

"So you created an alert out of spite, because I wanted evidence of my own before chasing someone through a casino?"

"In those words... yes. But additionally, it was clear she needed to be found, based on what she likely knows about this case. No offense, but I don't want to be chasing escaped prisoners for years, or even weeks. It's sometimes better to ask for forgiveness than permission for things like this, trust me."

"Oh brilliant. Was ignoring your chain of command a popular subject in your training classes at Leavenworth?"

"We're not ignoring anything. I'm sure you'll brief your higher-ups, like the good little spook you are, in due time. You're taking initiative on a road we would've eventually gone down anyway, since you were looking for her before this whole thing even started. What could go wrong?" Milo concluded with a sly grin.

"Yeah. Sure. Ask me again at my congressional hearing. So, mister daredevil. Where might this potential match be?

"The library, downtown. I've arranged for my car to be delivered at the south exit," he said getting up and stretching a bit.

"You don't want to see how Hyde fares for a bit first?"

"I'm not too worried about him. Besides, he has more room to distance himself from the hunter this time. I have a feeling we won't miss much."

"Eh, you've already gambled on one thing today. Why not pile on more?"

~

Alena was beginning to think she had picked the wrong place. Had she missed another obvious location to access the ComNet, or was Watson actually going to try and break into a military base? She knew all too well that desperation led to errors, often fatal ones in her former line of work. Somehow, that life has caught back up to her, and she understood that dozens of lives might hang in the balance. She had no intention of meeting with Watson in the manner that now befell her, considering they still had large strides to make in building trust, but one had to play the cards they were dealt, she regularly told herself. Besides, time was running out for one man as she sat waiting, and she was confident Rosen had already selected their next 'volunteer,' whomever that may be. The data Watson pulled from their archives was *vital* to how she would proceed, assuming his infiltration was a success.

Their method of communication to this point was via a secure, but seldom used, network designed for little more than text and short voice messages. Following the events at the Isard estate, they had agreed not to communicate until he was ready to transmit his bounty from the Network. Although she had been following the man, they had never met face-to-face, or talked live through voice or video. While the network could feasibly handle larger transmissions, she wasn't sure of the limits, and it would almost certainly tip off someone with the DOD, FBI, or Homeland Security, or all of the above. She couldn't take that risk, and she didn't have the luxury to wait for him to randomly portion off the data to suit his own agenda... assuming he had one.

Alena ran the scenarios in her mind for what seemed to her to be the hundredth time, and again came to the same conclusion. The only other possible way Watson could clandestinely access the military's ComNet in Reno, outside of a DOD installation, was from the public library. This wasn't a well-known fact, even in the upper echelons of government, though it did come in handy for field operatives in a pinch.

A great many libraries around the world had closed in the past few decades, usually those in smaller communities. However, the few hundred or so that survived made a concerted effort to become exceedingly innovative in a world that no longer maintained printed books. Alena tried to appear relaxed in the expansive, ultra-modern foyer of the downtown library, but that was proving difficult with the virtual librarian appearing every few minutes to offer assistance.

She found a modicum of success easing her agitated mind by focusing on the amenities available there. Apparently, aside from its vast digital archives, that particular location specialized in genealogy and migratory history of the entire western United States, rivaling museums and universities of the surrounding states, as well as the genealogical organizations in Utah. There were of course the standard conference rooms, web centers, and entertainment cubes that beleaguered most remaining libraries, but they all seemed to have an additional theme to set themselves apart from traditional facilities of generations past.

Her consideration of the mapping out of her family tree nearly caused her to miss two passersby entering the foyer. One was a middle-aged Latino woman in beige business attire; most likely going to a meeting in one of the state-of-the-art conference rooms, Alena guessed. The other was a somewhat younger Filipino man, who was noticeably fit, and wearing a muted gold-colored jacket with a Vegas Knights cap pulled low to his brow. Despite his subtle, yet effective-enough effort to conceal his identity from recognition scanners, Alena recognized Raymus Watson immediately.

Once both had passed through the open foyer, she let out a sigh of both relief and pent up angst. She was relieved to validate her long idle anticipation skills, proud they were still sharp. Conversely, she was apprehensive about how she was to approach the man she had only been messaging for a few weeks so as not send him underground again, or worse. She waited two full minutes, gathering her thoughts and mettle, then followed him to the web center pod on the sixth floor.

Chapter Fifteen: Dead Stop

Hal and Milo exited the car and exchanged furtive looks as they gazed upon the monumental building before them. "This is a *library*?" Hal wondered aloud.

The Reno Public Library was a tasteful amalgamation of old and new, though it ceased to give the impression of a traditional library long ago, Milo suspected. The first few floors of what appeared to be the original building, were an inexpensive, mid-twentieth century brown-brick, offset by narrow rows of vertical windows. More recent renovations added several more stories of mirrored glass in a triangular shape, placed on its side, giving it a semi-typical office building look.

They entered through the brick sides' main doors and were taken aback -- it seemed they had just stepped into the future. Nearly every horizontal and vertical surface had interactive displays, which were all the more pronounced by the soft mood lighting emanating from the floor and undersides of the plush form-chairs in each corner of the hexagonal room. Milo ventured farther into the foyer and a man appeared in front of him, prompting both men to reach for their sidearms.

"Good morning. My name is Vishnaré. I am your virtual tour guide at all public libraries in Nevada. How may I assist you today?"

Both hesitantly removed their hands from their respective gun handles and straightened back up. The male projection had a distinctly Native American look, but his name and complete lack of accent were somewhat of an enigma to the two men.

"Uh, hello. I'm Deputy US Marshal Milo Durron. I'm following up on a potential match of a Justice Department alert to a person of interest at this location, received approximately twenty minutes ago. Here are the details," Milo declared somewhat abashedly as he held up his folding tablet to the full-sized simulacrum.

Vishnaré shimmered some but didn't noticeably move. "Yes, Deputy Durron. That person shares a striking resemblance to a woman who sat in that chair, then proceeded to our web center through this door," he answered with a curtsy toward the appropriate door. "Shall I notify her of your arrival Deputy?"

"No, thank you. In fact I would appreciate you not communicating with or about her at all until further notice."

"Very well. Thank you for your patronage of the Nevada Public Library System." With that, Vishnaré vanished, and the lift to the web center opened conveniently with a soft hiss.

They arrived on the sixth floor and exited the cramped lift into a vast room surrounded entirely by windows, apart from the small entry alcove they stood in. The lift bank and restrooms were the focal point of the triangular floor layout, with only a customer service desk and sophisticated vending machine at the front to break up the dozens of rows of user cubicles. Milo quickly realized that doing a search of the massive floor on foot with only two people would be far too time consuming, until he looked to his distant left and observed what looked to be Watson having a heated conversation with a short-haired blonde woman.

"Excuse me," Milo boomed to the bored Indian teenager behind the customer service counter. Based on the hair and clothing style, he was taken aback to see a girl slowly look up, seemingly unimpressed by Milo's large stature. "Police, ma'am. How many exits are on this floor?"

The messy-haired girl wasn't interested in verifying Milo's credentials apparently, nor standing up while pointing out directions. "Besides the elevators? Um, there's stairs in each corner of the sono-cone... that's what we call the shape of this building."

"Good to know. Is it possible to block use of the lifts to and from this floor, temporarily?"

"Uh, I'll have to ask facilities management about that. Or maybe security...?"

"Do that, now please. There is an escaped prisoner on this floor and we need to limit his exits. Understand?" That revelation finally stimulated a mild emotional response, in the form of tented eyebrows. The inconvenienced girl nodded and turned to make the call. At the same moment, Milo spun to address Hal, but his partner was no longer behind him. For several manic seconds, he scanned the area searching, and his eyes finally landed on the man cavalierly making his way down the row closest to the glass wall on his left. He excitedly tapped behind his ear to reactivate his subdermal communicator.

"Would you mind telling me your plan again? I must've forgotten that whole conversation we didn't have," Milo said through gritted teeth.

"Take it easy. They don't know what we look like. We can't just go right toward them, they'll make a run for it. I'm trying to get on the other side of them as non-threateningly as I can so we can box them in. Besides, I'm fairly certain the person Watson is talking with is Alena Sarne. How much more convenient for us could it be?"

"They're not some feral animals we're trying to cage and donate to a zoo," Milo reminded. "They're highly trained intelligence agents, or at least Watson is. Besides, there's a chance he got a look at us earlier in the…"

Milo stopped short when he saw Watson taking off at a sprint in the direction of the nearest stairwell. While Hal was much closer to the man, he knew he'd never be able to catch him. "He's on the move! Make yourself useful and get acquainted with her will ya? I'm gonna try and cut him off."

"How? Do you have superpowers you haven't mentioned before? He's already at the stairwell!"

"None that would help us here," Milo quipped. "But I do have a car on remote that can track him through the glass once I lock on to him." As he dashed for the elevator, he flipped open his tablet and fired up the car's remote app. Despite it being a top-of-the-line American luxury vehicle, it didn't have much in the way of a surveillance package... or, more accurately, none whatsoever. It did however have a 'find and follow' feature typically used when an owner or renter doesn't need a vehicle right away, but may need one at a moment's notice. It can also be programed to follow another person for the same reasons once it locks on to their profile.

The girl behind the desk was still on the phone with someone, so he was able to access the lift without delay. Milo swiftly waded through the technology-packed foyer and out the main doors. The mid-morning sun was already warming up the dry October air. The image on his tablet showed his car was approaching the glass-enclosed stairwell. He was thrilled to see that Watson was still inside, but nearly ran into a post allowing himself a moment to chortle at his good fortune.

His Studebaker tracked Watson as he bounded down flights of steps four at a time. He had reached the bottom and burst out of the emergency exit as if he were running from fire. Since the Skyhawk wasn't a police vehicle, it had none of the standard equipment an interceptor does, so Milo simply had the vehicle follow the man until the opportunity to be reunited with it presented itself. For now he was running down the sidewalk glued to his tablet; not too strange a sight to garner much attention.

"How's it going up there?" He asked through his subdermal communicator, somewhat winded.

"Oh, um... good. Forgot you were there actually. We're briefing each other with a healthy dose of contrition, but I'll probably have to do a warm hand-off somewhere for her safety. How are things going on your end?"

"I'm pursuing on foot while watching him carjack someone through my find and follow function. So all-in-all, it could be better. I didn't want to have to do this, but I need to call this in before that woman who just had her car stolen does, and it comes out later that I did nothing to assist. This is the sort of thing that ruins promotion potential."

Milo heard the inductions of a protest from Hal, but switching channels to an emergency line cut the man off. Milo identified himself, and explained the situation to the dispatcher, as calmly as he could while still at a hasty jog. "He's headed north, approaching the Virginia Street Bridge in a tan Packard. I'm in pursuit but requesting a vehicle deactivation." The dispatcher acknowledged the request, but didn't pledge action just yet. The owner of the soft, yet confident female voice was likely conferring with a supervisor, as well as locating nearby patrol units, Milo supposed.

Remote vehicle deactivations were relatively common and harmless police actions that involved a forced shutdown on civilian cars. Through a series of codes, transmitted from various points around metropolitan centers, or from satellites in unincorporated areas, cars are essentially rendered unusable by turning off the electronics and mechanically locking the driver inside the vehicle. Another code, transmitted to responding officers, allows them to unlock the downed vehicle at their discretion.

Having more eyes on the stolen car allowed Milo to halt his foot pursuit. He was finally back in his Stude and speeding after Watson when his mobile came alive once more. "Deputy Durron, deactivation has been authorized. There are two units approaching the vehicle from the north end of the bridge. Shutdown signal will be sent when they are within fifty meters."

"Copy dispatch. Please advise your units to contain *only*. It is imperative that the driver be placed into my custody." Milo held his tongue in providing any more specific information on Watson. He dared not use words like 'dangerous' or 'fugitive' as their use might change the nature of police response protocol.

The scene unfolded in front of him within seconds. The stolen Packard was canted across the bridge, blocking traffic from both directions, with one police air bike hovering a few meters away from the driver's side door. The other was keeping southbound traffic at a safe distance. Milo was coming in for a soft landing far behind where Watson sat besieged when a loud pop made him slam on the brakes. He sat, suspended in midair, staring in awe at the spectacle before him.

Somehow, Watson had managed to activate the emergency door release, propelling it clear from the car by several compressed air pockets within the frame, and striking the air bike with enough force to knock the officer from his perch.

Before the air bike, as well as the officer, stopped moving, Watson was out of the Packard, sprinting straight toward the downed police vehicle. Milo knew that with the speed and maneuverability of an air bike, Watson would be nearly impossible to catch, so he piloted the Studebaker to intercept. The other Reno PD officer had also heard the door exploding and was racing to assist her fallen comrade.

Milo was preparing to take position directly over the air bike when he witnessed Watson freeze in his tracks, and dramatically slump onto the street like a marionette with its strings cut. Milo drifted the car to the right and keenly watched Watson's limp body for any sign of movement. Once he was content that it wasn't a ruse, he landed to investigate further.

As Milo approached the motionless form lying next to the inert air bike, he was challenged by the uninjured police officer. He identified himself and presented his credentials. After vacillating between him and his shiny new car, she was apparently satisfied enough to focus her efforts on her dismounted counterpart.

Watson appeared to be peacefully sleeping at first glance. Milo advanced with his weapon drawn, in case the man had another trick up his proverbial sleeve. He nudged him with his foot and Watson flopped over onto his back like a rag doll. A quick inspection revealed no obvious signs of injury. Milo was turning to address the officer when he noticed a small pool of blood under the still figure's head, so he circled around to locate its source.

He eventually saw that blood had trickled from the right ear and eye, with the left eye looking disturbingly blood-shot as well. Milo straightened back up and sighed as he re-holstered his sidearm, thoroughly convinced it was not an act.

~

Sonya watched the slow-paced cat and mouse game from a large assembly room, aptly named the 'hunters den' over the years. The space was both a training area and sparring arena to test the hunters' mettle. There was a raised observation room set aside with modest seating, and a full view of the open area for trainers and other spectators to watch the goings-on, or judge any scored matches. The dull, beige room was considerably brighter and more comfortable than the training area, but whenever Sonya was in the Rosen building she spent nearly her entire visit in one or another corner of the den. Many of the hunters in fact could only be found there when in the building.

The second round of The Game was not quite as enthralling as the first. Prisoner 74205 had shot down two of the four seekers and continued to make his way to the nearest safety ring, she guessed. She was certain Jack assumed as much, since it appeared to her that he was rushing to get ahead of his prey in the bowl-shaped zone.

Sonya watched, hoping both for action and for 74... Hyde, to make it in one piece to the safety ring; knowing only one of those was going to happen. A blue light illuminated on the armrest of the chaise she currently inhabited, indicating an incoming internal call. "This is Kane, go."

"Ah yes, Ms. Kane. Mr. Hoberd can see you now in his office... if it's a convenient time for you that is?"

"Tell Joe I'll be right up," she interjected, promptly closing the channel on the procurement office assistant. She leapt up gracefully and made her way to the nearest lift. Jovan Hoberd, the Director of Asset Procurement, was a very quiet, shy, fortyish man who had a bit of a crush on Sonya. They only saw each other in passing every so often, but his puppy dog expressions gave him away at their first encounter. She intended to use that to her advantage.

Sonya strode into the third floor office as if it were her own, walked right by the assistant whose name she could never remember, and sat in the form-chair facing Jovan's desk like they were old acquaintances. "Making me wait almost two hours Joe? I thought we were friends?"

The man was utterly flabbergasted. "I, uh... you've never been to my office before," he stammered. "I was in the middle of something, plus I wasn't sure it was a genuine request. What brings you up here anyway?" he asked, regaining some composure though barely looking her in the eye.

"Well, with a welcome like that..." she teased. "I have a problem I was hoping you can help me with."

"Yes?" he breathed, heavy with desire.

"I'd be ever so grateful if you'd permit a couple friends of mine to talk to you about the process of acquiring network contestants."

"Oh," he huffed disappointedly, slumping into his plush leather seat that was much bigger than he was. "No I'm afraid not. I can't even discuss that process with *you*, let alone outsiders."

Sonya leaned forward, and in a flinty voice said, "Not even me? Are you sure Joe? I can be *very* persuasive if I have to be, you know."

A dark, stern look crossed over the man's face. She couldn't tell if it was an attempt at confidence, or if he was afraid of what he was about to say.

"Quite sure. In fact, Sonya, it's been made abundantly clear to me that anyone not authorized to have information regarding this office are to be reported immediately, or face termination and legal action. I'm sorry to say that you are not on that very short authorization list. As much as I... respect you, I like my job and livelihood more."

"Wait, what?" Sonya asked, dropping the siren routine. "You're gonna report me for taking an interest in how the company finds my opponents?"

"I'm afraid so. I don't have much choice in the matter now, since at least two people here know we're talking. I doubt you're in much danger of punitive measures, but I certainly am. Perhaps next time we chat will be under more cordial circumstances. Good day Sonya."

With that, she departed Joe's office to head back down to the den, feeling something she had never felt before. Was she just rejected? Or was the numb, disassociated feeling from guilt, for attempting to grift someone into doing her bidding, placing all the risk upon him? No, she thought. Definitely not guilt.

Chapter Sixteen: Zenith

Milo stood staring at the triage medical extractor as it loudly, but quickly, ascended to its cruising altitude and sped away to the nearest military hospital with the body of Raymus Watson. He watched until the craft had been swallowed up by the blue autumn sky, completely oblivious of Hal and Alena approaching solemnly from behind.

Hal took a position next to him, mimicking his thoughtful pose. After a long moment he asked, "What did the Timmy doc say?"

"Massive brain hemorrhage. Almost as if a small bomb went off inside his head. The medical resident shared her findings with a couple of other doctors. She'd never seen anything like it before," came Milo's monotone response without looking over toward his partner.

Hal nodded unconsciously. He had tried to warn him, but the old network they were communicating on had a limited range, and he wasn't fast enough to look up Milo's mobile number in time to convey his warning. For several seconds they both stood watching a fixed point in the sky, which was now empty. Finally, Hal decided to tell the man what he knew about their mutual fugitives.

"Since a sizable number of people implanted with an ASI often developed psychological issues, a sort-of failsafe was designed to protect the chain of command, and the general public. It works as a self-destruct in a way, by overloading the implant. The catch to that is you have to know a person's exact location, down to a few meters, for it to be enabled."

Milo bowed his head at the realization. "And by calling the police I just handed over that location, because all cops have an accessible GPS tracker as a regular part of their uniform. They also transmit regular updates through police radio traffic, which is even easier to tap into."

"Whoa, whoa! You didn't know. Don't beat yourself up over doing what you thought was right. Besides, as smart as Watson was, I figured he found some way to alter his implant, or at least that particular feature... assuming he even knew about it that is," Hal said, attempting to reassure the man. It didn't seem to work though, as Milo turned and stared intently at him.

"Who would've made that call? To activate Watson's failsafe? And why now? Why not when he was at Leavenworth, or when he got picked up after Belarus? You didn't fill me in on the off-switch, can you at least humor me by answering those?"

Hal was stung by that last comment but tried to not let it show. "Best guess, someone affiliated with Rosen pulled the plug after Watson outlived his usefulness with them. It wasn't all in vain though. He uncovered some encouraging data on them that could put a nice bow on our mission..."

"*Our* mission?" Milo interjected exasperatedly. "I hate to break it to you pal, but I'm not on any mission. *I'm* working a sanctioned OP with the code-name of Rubicon to retrieve three escapees, two of whom died right in front of me and the third may as well be dead. The way I see it, my part here is over."

Hal stood motionless, dumbfounded by what he just heard. Although their time together had been short, he thought he had gotten through to Milo to empathize with his fellow veterans. A bona fide confidant to partner with in the lonely life of espionage. But perhaps he underestimated fracturing the loyalty of the career government employee.

"Do you think that name was chosen at random? I'm sure I don't have to tell you the significance of the phrase 'crossing the Rubicon.' But in case you missed the subtle pronouncement, your so-called 'sanctioned OP' was Colonel Takbrite's transition from a respected Army officer, to an asset in Rosen's pocket. Him bringing on the Marshals was just a ploy to aid in leading those goons in red to the fugitives, and appease anyone else who may be watching the situation unfold."

"How do you *know* that? Still keeping things from me huh? That tactic may have worked to bait your hook before, but it's wearing a bit thin..."

"No! No, that's not what's happening here. Although I suspected he was into something unbecoming, I didn't know the extent of his machinations until Alena informed me not fifteen minutes ago. He didn't do this alone; he was simply an integral piece of the meticulously conceived plan by Rosen. Speaking of which, there's still time to help Marcus, but we have to act quickly. Our chances of success go up with your help. But I'll understand if you want to part ways here."

For several long moments Milo contemplated the offer. He could walk away right now with his hands clean of the whole affair, from both a legal and professional perspective. However, he knew himself. Despite being a life-long soldier, and celebrated instructor of Army doctrine, he was not unsympathetic to the moments where countermanding orders was the right thing to do. If there was anything to be done that could either help Hyde, or clear his name, his conscience wouldn't allow him to simply leave, hands clean or not.

"All right. Say I happen to stick around a bit longer; there will be a few conditions. I'll want full disclosure on what the both of you know about Rosen, ASIs, and any data connecting them to your overall mission. Secondly, I want to be the one to make whatever command decisions may come our way from here on out, since I'm the only person here who has any legitimate authority. So to start things off on the right foot, what would my contribution entail exactly? How do we get Hyde out of the zone in time with a few articles of dirty laundry?"

"It's much more than that," Alena spoke up. "The data Watson uncovered strikes directly at Rosen's wallet; against people who would rather not be outed as backers. Not to mention shining a very bright light on some of their questionable recruitment methods, and overall shady dealings both here and abroad."

"Sounds good. What do you need me for then?"

"Because of what Marcus said at the end of the first round," Hal offered. "'As the sun makes its zenith, so must I,' Alena thinks, he's referring to the long-considered defunct Zenith Electronics company..."

"So, what? They're going to invent the remote control again? You're not selling this very well doc."

"My pessimism is wearing off on you. No, Watson must've told the others that the zone hard line comms network is of older Zenith tech, which is historically known to be susceptible to military-grade communicators, including implanted personal ones."

Milo stared at the man for a long moment. Hal's point had finally clicked. "We can find him, *and* talk to him!" He said with a newfound zeal. Then his analytical side took back over. "Why didn't Watson try to find him if he knew about the network's backdoor? If that was the reason he came here..."

"It wasn't," Alena interjected, tired of being left out of the conversation. She was shorter than the two men, but lithe and had the hard look of someone who had given and received difficult orders in her thirty-something years. "Raymus was here on my request to infiltrate Rosen, which he successfully accomplished early this morning. I also advised against attempting to contact Hyde as to avoid potentially giving away his position, as well as telegraphing his intentions."

Milo was confused again. "So... Watson worked for you? Were you his handler, or whatever you call it?" He asked with a surly grin toward Hal.

"Not exactly. Er, not at all for the first part. When DIA asked me to look into Corrections' contracts with Rosen, it didn't take me long to see something was fishy; only a few hours really. I then hacked into their meager, yet still impressive, messaging network because all other ways in were too well protected. From there I was able to glean a reasonably clear picture of the extent of their field operatives' configuration."

"And that means what to us, exactly?" Milo asked somewhat loudly. "This pseudo-spy stuff is not as charming as you might think. It's been quite a few years since someone has died right in front of me. So you'll excuse me if I *strongly* encourage you two to cut to the chase."

"Message received," Alena responded while holding her hands up, acquiescing. "I figured out Rosen wanted people with ASIs, either as hunters or prey. They tried to recruit Watson while on assignment in Belarus, but because he didn't commit to them right away they moved to discredit and frame him so he could get arrested, taking the choice away from him altogether. I warned him it would happen after their first meeting. He didn't trust me then, but his experiences following that so-called escape gave him a different perspective."

"Which led to his brain exploding. What I'm interested in is what he... now you, have on Rosen, aside from a few confidential sponsors, that would cause them to make a call like that? To allegedly kill a man in public, who wasn't even on the Network."

"Pretty much all of the classified governmental funding that, if not kept secret, would fundamentally ruin their reputation as a company, along with the careers of some powerful figures. It would render their most popular, and therefore profitable, programming unsustainable literally overnight. Not to mention expose several officials and business executives as taking kickbacks, or worse."

"Which brings us back to why the hell I shouldn't get back to my cozy job halfway across the country! You say this OP was a farce from the beginning? Great, you sold me on that. Job well done. But I took it seriously, and it was a qualified disaster. So for me, it's on to the next one. I wish you both luck in your endeavors."

"Milo wait," Hal pleaded as he grabbed Milo's arm. Milo looked at the clutched arm, then gave a hard glare into the other man's blue-grey eyes, which prompted a quick release. "Sorry, but it's not as simple as that. According to what Watson dug up from Rosen's archives, they have set their sights on your office, amongst *many* others. You, and three of your colleagues, were specifically chosen for Rubicon to test your mettle against highly sought assets. You were obviously the standout winner."

Milo vacillated between the two spies with incredulity, waiting for one to break their composure. When neither gave in he took on a sarcastic tone. "Oh I see. Their big, evil plan was to make me a runner in the Game. I can see it now, the oldest contestant to ever grace the Network."

"Not exactly," Alena cut in. "They were going to offer you a field recruitment position; likely due to your discipline and dependability if I had to guess. If you had turned them down, which it seems they expect you to, they plan to either discredit you via your beloved car, or somehow tie you into the fiasco that took place in Manchuria during the war…"

"That's classified information!" Milo exploded in a fury. "There's simply not enough evidence to pin *any* of that calamity on me, mainly due to the *fact* that no such information exists!"

"Yeah, well, that's kinda the point we're trying to make isn't it," Hal said. "With their growing number of contacts within DOD, they could've gathered just enough data on you to make up whatever they wanted and have it sound credible. Then blackmail you to comply, either as a staff member or contestant in one of their many, and I use this term *very* loosely, reality shows."

"But why bother when they have the money, and influence, to recruit whomever they want? Why would they waste their time on people who clearly aren't interested?"

"Because Rosen doesn't target just anybody. They don't settle for runner-up. Also, apparently their sales pitch comprises a fair amount of intellectual property that could damage their recruitment process if released. Not to mention that, as a company, they're completely narcissistic," Alena informed.

The anger rising within Milo was reaching a point he had not felt for many years. Most probably as far back as that ill-fated military operation that became known as the Manchurian Catastrophe, where he assumed command of what remained of an entire company, in what was supposed to be a safe zone. He swallowed down the bile and focused on a solution like he always did in situations such as these.

"So what are you proposing we do about this? Especially since you seem to already have the intel you need to break their back."

"We need someone on the inside," Alena chimed in. "I mean physically. We need you to go inside the zone and connect with the Zenith network, to aid in creating a backdoor into their larger system. If we can do that, we can transmit our data through Rosen's own streaming services, which will reach far more people than a news station or public streaming channels that only niche groups will see.

Milo scoffed and waved off the notion as if it were a buzzing pest. "That's all well and good lady, but the zone security net will have locked onto me long before I get anywhere near enough to connect to anything... unless you have a cloaking device up your sleeve?" He concluded mockingly.

"Not exactly," she responded in what was becoming her usual phrase. She was either not impressed by the joke, or oblivious to the reference; Milo couldn't tell. "However, we do have access to a few of Rosen's vehicle transponders. It may not fool them for long, but long enough to hack in and block their zone security..."

The two men waited for her to continue what appeared to be an unfinished thought. When no elaboration came, Milo broke the silence that ensued.

"Um, ok. Just like that? Anything else I can do for you two?"

"Yes, you might want to contact that friend of yours who works for Rosen, and get her to do anything she can to help us, just in case their response time is faster than I anticipate. Oh, and you should probably try to contact Mister Hyde while you're in the zone. You should be able to reach him through the Zenith network, potentially rendering assistance if possible."

Milo's head snapped to his left to face Hal. By the grimace on the other man's face, it was clear he had forgotten about Hyde as well. They raced to Milo's car, almost knocking Alena over in the process.

"Do you think it's over yet?" An already winded Hal asked.

"Dammit man! Don't say it like that."

They reached the Studebaker at the same time, and Milo activated the view-screen. He directed his onboard computer to the Rosen Network, but paused to regard Hal.

"You might want to make this your port of call sailor. It didn't sound like I have time to chauffeur you around at the moment."

The Most Dangerous Game appeared superimposed across the center of the windscreen, leaving an adequate amount of unimpeded visibility for the driver and passenger. The image briefly captivating the both of them was of Marcus carefully navigating a heavily rocky terrain. Towering granite formations surrounded the intrepid contestant. He methodically scanned each crack and crevice for anything out of the ordinary. Both men let out a relieved sigh.

"And let you go charging to the rescue alone? I couldn't allow myself to miss that, especially since I got you into this in the first place," Hal added sheepishly. "Besides, between piloting this thing, attempting to access the network, coordinating with Alena, and contacting Marcus I figure you could use an extra pair of finely tuned surgeon hands."

"Oh that's right, you're a doctor," Milo responded dramatically. "Perhaps you might be able to finally use those skills in this tactical infiltration operation."

"Funny. Now get us in the air while I try to contact Sonya. Hopefully Marcus can hang in there a bit longer."

"My money is still on another victory. Maybe it's good that I'm allowing you to tag along though, in case he really *will* need a doctor."

Chapter Seventeen: Coup de Grâce

Senior Airman Marcus Hyde was beginning to go mad. Even though he knew there was only one enemy out there, he perceived threats with every unidentified sound, and every sway of desert grass.

He consulted his forearm datapad, which held preloaded information such as: detailed maps of the zones, date and time, as well as known inventory, amongst other applicable information. The catch to this fairly standard, toned-down military equipment is that, for the purposes of the Game, at least one piece of data had to be entered into every application offered through the computer. He checked his location, based on the position he calculated in between rounds, and his computer-estimated position put him slightly under two kilometers southwest of a safety ring...

There was a faint, metallic scraping to his distant right that caused Marcus to reflexively go prone onto the ground, huddled behind his small duffel bag. Although he was well aware of the strands of titanium and spider-silk threads of body armor sewn within his battle dress uniform, it wouldn't protect him from the concussive force of average munitions. What saved most soldiers' lives in battle was the powered combat vest, or PCV. Through the use of repulse technology, the battery-powered vest essentially pushed back on impacts severe enough to cause moderate injury, with the help of the hardened outer layer of material electronically stiffened to absorb the kinetic energy.

Thanks to dozens of tiny solar cells, which were also part of the PCV, the battery could continually charge in the warm Nevada sun. The vest's battery also powered the forearm datapad, as well as the integrated helmet and environmental mask, both inundated with several features of their own. Despite those touted and tested benefits, he still had the impulse to use his equipment bag as a shield.

Straining his senses for another sound, or movement of any kind, Marcus could feel his muscles tensing. Readying themselves for the instinctive fight or flight response that even experienced soldiers still had to contend with. As he stood there, still as the stones around him, he quietly berated himself for not exiting the shallow valley he had entered in hopes of evading the seekers. While that decision was one of strategic necessity, it may have allowed the hunter to gain ground on him more quickly.

Seconds stretched by, as if time were standing still. After several breathless moments, Marcus relaxed some and thought it best to at least put on his helmet. As he twisted his body to reach for the helmet strapped to his vest on the left side, the rock wall behind him exploded in a muffled pop, showering him with sand and stone.

Marcus slapped the Kevlar helmet on his head and scurried back the way he had come. He fired off a few controlled bursts in the direction his gut told him the threat was coming from, but received no definitive hits in response to his efforts. When the echoes from his weapon's staccato sounds faded, Marcus clearly heard a soft hiss and smooth action noises from a well-oiled pneumatic re-loader, which in his mind narrowed the possible weapon of his assailant down to a silenced SPAS-22 shotgun, or an auto bow.

He continued to incrementally stretch the distance between himself and his attacker. Without taking his eyes off the narrow valley before him, Marcus desperately tried to remember the layout of the area he had just traversed only minutes ago. He knew there was a small crevasse on his left that could not only provide adequate cover, but also a path to higher ground. He was certain it was close, and was getting frustrated by not seeing...

An intense force struck him square in his stomach, propelling him off his feet. The PCV had done its job and absorbed the brunt of the impact, but he was still lying flat on his back with the wind knocked out of him. He dared not sit up, for fear the same weapon came for his head, so he tried scanning the area where he lay. As he writhed on the ground, his breath returning to him, his strength came back in a jolt when he saw the rocky fissure he had been searching for looming behind him.

Seemingly in one swift motion, Marcus rolled to his left, and deftly slithered along the valley wall, into the cleft of rock. As he tucked his legs inside, the blur of an arrow darted by and struck the opposite wall. The specially designed bolt head had a series of barbed hooks packed within it, no doubt meant to incapacitate limbs, he assumed.

He clamored his way to the top of the stunted valley and tossed a smoke grenade in the direction of his attacker. The still air and depressed features of the area ensured maximum coverage of the heavy grey fog. For good measure, he lobbed a timed flechette grenade to the far end of the cloud, and took off at a sprint toward the safety ring. At the pace he was moving, Marcus could easily make the safety ring in five minutes, give or take. Unfortunately, due to the rough terrain, and the fact he couldn't maintain his current pace with all his gear, the trip would likely take up to eight, he cursorily calculated.

The boom of the second grenade echoed across the area like a firecracker, followed shortly by a muffled grunt. Marcus spun toward the sound and fired into the dissipating cloud. Again, there was no clear reply to his shots, as if the bullets were swallowed up by the smoke. He leapt up with a jolt and resumed his flight.

He pushed his body to its limit. His lungs burned, and his legs were stiff and heavy, like they were made of petrified wood. He had lost track of time, and wasn't entirely certain he was still going the right direction.

Marcus was about to slow down to consult his datapad when he saw it. The golden glow of the safety ring beckoned him like a soul to heaven. He mustered all the strength he had left and sprinted toward the artificial enclave that housed his salvation.

As he rapidly approached the ring, a sudden, intense pain pierced his lower torso. He felt himself slowing, no matter how much he willed to move onward. Finally, he had to drop to his knee and saw the cause of his plight. The long bolt of an auto-bow was protruding from his abdomen. The head of the arrow was unfamiliar, but it had opened up like a flower, with the petals flush against his skin. In the center there was also the unmistakable arching of electrodes feeding into the metallic petals.

"It's sapping your will," a raspy, Australian voice pronounced behind him. "That's why you're slowly weakening. That's why this hunt will be known as the one that *almost* got away."

Marcus plopped down onto the dirt while turning to face his attacker. The man before him was tall, but not overly imposing. He presumed it was because the figure was aesthetically conservative by employing very little gear, though the sad state he approached was also a contender. The hunter wore impressive adaptive camouflage, but parts of it along the right side weren't working, and seemed to be stuck on a dull grey color. Upon closer inspection, Marcus noticed a few tenacious, spiked flechettes from his grenade peeking out of the damaged suit. A sense of sullen satisfaction washed over him like a shadow, and became apparent to the man standing over him.

"Yes, it was a good lob. I managed to pull out some, but a few of the buggers are in deep. My hat goes off to you mate. I've never been injured during a hunt before. Now then, any last words?"

Marcus stared at him with burning contempt. The Aussie's nonchalance about killing someone he didn't even know was appalling. The way he stood oozed arrogance as well, like he was putting on a show and figured he was already out of danger. Marcus racked his brain to come up with something witty to say. When nothing to his liking came to him, he figured snide was the way to go.

"Yeah. I do. You should really ask to see the hands of a person you're about to kill before taunting them. It kinda damages the mystique when it backfires."

A confused mien crossed Jack's face. Then one of panicked realization. As fast as he was, it made no difference to an opponent who was already prepared to strike. Marcus depressed the trigger of the ballistic knife hidden behind his leg. The blade shot out like one of Jack's bow bolts and hit its target in the throat.

Two heavy spurts of blood were ejected before the hunter attempted to quell the flow with his hand, but it had been too late. His hand turned crimson in seconds, which loosened his grip on the gushing wound. Marcus had drawn his sidearm immediately after he fired the knife, though he now knew it wouldn't be needed.

Jack collapsed mere centimeters from where Marcus sat, blood pooling beneath him rapidly. While not nearly as severe, Marcus turned his attention to his own injury. The bolt had run out of power, but he couldn't feel his strength returning, and every move he made sent stabbing pain across his body. Something needed to be done, and soon, or he ran the risk of becoming septic and joining the man laying next him.

He knew Network medics would be sent to patch him up before the next round. Because contestants in live shows were essentially investment property, there was little in the way of medical equipment issued.

However, he was unsure of their response time, since injured participants were treated off screen. He rummaged through the duffel and pulled out a laser wire cutter. While it was designed to cut through optical cable, and the occasional circuit board, Marcus knew it had been tested well beyond those levels, and was certain the polymer-alloy material of the arrow would be no problem.

In seconds, the bolt head had been seared off, and the remainder of the projectile was gingerly eased out through his back. This effort solved one problem, yet caused another. He now had two gaping holes in his body, far too close to vital organs for comfort. He didn't have the dexterity to perform any precise surgery on his back, so he slapped a proderm patch over it, from the limited supply he carried, and concentrated on his abdomen wound.

Marcus knew he had to work fast, because his vision was blurring and he was becoming light-headed from the blood loss. He poured the remainder of his canteen over the hole just below his liver to get a better look at what he had to work with. He dabbed the area with torn fabric from his shirt and pinched the hole as best he could. With a shaking hand, and sweat pouring off his face, Marcus cauterized the wound with the laser wire cutter. Without anesthetic, and a steady hand, the pain was unbearable. He wished he had something to bite on, but it was over in the longest seconds he'd ever experienced. He slapped his last proderm patch on the area and passed out, in a very uncomfortable posture next to the still twitching hunter.

~

Marcus awoke to the hot afternoon sky, beckoning him to another horizon. Even though he wasn't a pilot, he loved being in the air, or at the very least off the ground. It had been ages since he had flown, but this was a different sensation entirely. He may be delirious, but he had the distinct feeling the clouds were moving, in the opposite direction they were traveling just a moment ago.

A wave of dizziness swept over him. His body was being held in place by restraints. Through immense strain he was able to turn his head slightly to see two men guiding the stretcher he laid upon to what looked to be a shiny, new triage medical extractor, or as his ilk liked to call them, a Timmy. He rested his head back down to face the sky, relief easing the tension in his neck and shoulders.

In what felt like hours, Marcus's head began to clear, the pain fading like the drifting clouds he had focused on as he fell unconscious the second time. He lay on his stomach and could hear the whirr of the mechanical arms, still working on his back injury he supposed. He could also hear one of the medics arguing with someone via the telepresence system that allows anyone present to confer with practitioners.

"Negative. I can't guarantee how leaving a dead kidney in the body will affect his performance. Nor do I recommend waiting on installing a new one. The damage to his spleen has been repaired, and he mitigated further tissue damage when he cauterized himself with a laser cutter, but he can be transported to the med station and back in less than an hour in a *much* better condition... to assuage any question of fairness that may come up by our loyal fan base."

"I get what you're saying," the feminine voice on the other end began, "but you know how they'll respond if I forward your request. 'It's an acceptable loss, leaving essential functionality intact,' they'll say. Besides, he still has one good kidney, and he may not even need that one for long anyway."

The man in the TME sighed heavily. "Your misanthropic attitude notwithstanding, the man just won his second round, in spectacular fashion I might add. I think he's earned a little optimism in surviving the third. Could you humor me by at least asking? A little empathy in our line of work hasn't been completely depleted yet, has it?"

"Very well. Stand by please," the woman responded before switching off her screen; seemingly unaffected by the man's question of morality.

"Nicely done, doctor," the other man said. The voice startled Marcus. Not only because the source was coming from right next to him and he hadn't noticed the man standing there, leaning against some storage bins, but also because he was certain he recognized it. He forced his eyes to focus on the tall figure. The man nodded cordially, and Marcus couldn't decide if he should be relieved or incredibly worried.

"You guys just can't get enough of me can you?" he asked, feeling more groggy than he sounded.

Milo smiled, and continued focusing on a tablet he tapped every few seconds. "Can you blame us? We're trying to get you out of here kid, but we're not out of the woods yet."

"Anything?" Hal asked apprehensively.

"Nothing. And please stop asking. You have a patient to attend to anyway, one we might need to move under his own power very soon. How much of what you told that machine posing as a woman was true?"

"What're you guys talking about? How did you get here?" Marcus interrupted, feeling his vigor returning. The mechanical arms had recessed back into the ceiling. He tried to sit up, Hal gently preventing him.

"It's pretty simple really," Milo volunteered, a proud smirk slipping through his faux-stern façade. "We caught up with the source Watson was getting his intel and marching orders from. She told us about the old zone network. Then, since our contact inside Rosen didn't answer her phone, we had to come up with our own way to get close enough in order to hack into that system. Mister super-spy here came up with the idea of commandeering a Timmy at the nearest med station, allowing us to kill two birds with one stone... the second being finding a way to get you out. Questions?"

Marcus traded stares between both men, gauging their seriousness. He couldn't tell if they were joking, crazy, or both, so he just went with it and left the details alone.

"Uh, when you put it like that, I suppose not. So... what's the plan from here?"

"That sounds like a question to me," Milo retorted. "We're waiting to get word about the hack. Or for Rosen to grow some integrity, and either allow us to take you to a medical facility, or let actual law enforcement take care of you. Whichever comes first. Either way, be prepared to..."

Relentless beeping from his tablet cut him off. Milo resumed his dour perusing of the screen, while the other two stared in anticipation. After what seemed far too long to process what he was reading, he looked up to two pairs of wide eyes.

"Oh, sorry. We're in business. I was just reading the particulars, but I suppose that's not as important as us getting the hell out of here. I'll drive."

Milo dashed into the only seat of what service members referred to as the cockpit, since the piloting and overall shape of the Timmys had more in common with commercial aircraft than standard military or emergency vehicles. They're also designed to travel quite fast, due to the impetuous nature of their passengers. He fired up the engines and took off as if they were shot out of a cannon. He stayed low to the ground however, in hopes of confusing any tracking equipment that may be used against them. Almost immediately after takeoff, monitors came to life all over the craft.

"Medical shuttle two-eight-two, you have not been authorized to return to base. What are your intentions, over?"

All three men exchanged glances. Hal shrugged his shoulders and responded. "Control, this is 282. We have a medical emergency on our hands, and our patient can't wait for the situation to be discussed by a committee."

"Understood doctor, but it has been determined that prisoner 74205's identified injuries do not require further attention…"

"Oh? When was this going to be shared with *us*? I reported that he was already prepped. That's not a condition where we can sit around twiddling our thumbs."

The new person on the other end took on a haughty expression. "You're getting the message when the decision was made, doctor… I didn't catch your name and operating number."

Hal opened his mouth to respond when all the screens with the angry man's face went dark. He looked over at Milo and saw a glimmer of satisfaction from his over-the-shoulder profile glance.

"Sorry, but it's probably best we don't engage with anyone. Especially those of us who have a job to worry about... One that won't have my back if I get caught conducting some good old-fashioned corporate theft and espionage."

"Yeah, I think I get the picture," Hal remarked snidely. "You undoubtedly just saved me from an impending boring conversation anyway. So, what should we expect them to throw at us? Can we assume they'll let us go with an unconditional surrender?"

"Don't hold your breath. They're probably trying a remote shut down right now. If Alena's efforts are as debilitating as she claimed, they won't be able to do that, or coordinate with any of the zone's automated systems. Since we're still moving, I'll wager a guess it's at least a partial success. So what they'll do next, I assume, is send *manned* security craft to intercept us. Recycled patrol craft from the war, if you recall seeing those cloud cars docked at the other side of the landing pad from the Timmys."

"If they're anything like the ones at the colonies," Marcus cut in, "those can pack some serious firepower."

"Maybe it's wishful thinking, but I kinda doubt Rosen has access to that level of weaponry." Milo said, not fully convinced of his own assurances. "They are however of the same class of craft, I suspect. Doc, if there's anything else you need to do to get ready for a chase, now's the time to get creative."

Milo banked the TME hard to starboard. They were now heading due east, instead of northwest where the zone medical facility sat.

"Where do you have us headed now?" Hal wondered. "I didn't think going the opposite direction was what you meant by getting 'creative.'"

"We need to get out of Rosen territory; east is the shortest route from Zone Jupiter. Isn't that right Marcus?"

"Um, yeah, I think so. How would *you* know that though?"

"Sorry son, trade secrets. If I told you I'd have to kill you. Though since that threat obviously doesn't that bothers you, give me a minute to think of a less clichéd one."

Chapter Eighteen: Endgame

Sonya left the Game Master's office in a huff. Although she was expecting to be passed over for Hyde's third round, given what the man classified as 'lapses in professionalism,' it was still an upsetting decision. She had never been snubbed for *anything* in her entire professional career. To make matters worse, it had been the second time she'd been denied that day!

She roamed the hallways of the Network building in a haze of anger and disappointment. This had all started when I received those anonymous messages a few weeks ago, she blamed. She had an enviable job that didn't give her a moment's pause, until what she first assumed was creepy fan mail had somehow found its way into her inbox. Since then, she had taken a look at her life and realized how lonely she truly was. She also began questioning if Rosen was the ethically responsible company they appeared to be when she was recruited into their ranks.

At that moment, a soft alarm was activated. It gave off the distinct tone of the keys of a large xylophone being played at a slow, steady tempo. Sonya laughed to herself, thinking that noise would never inspire anyone to take action. What the alarm did succeed in however, was to snap her out of her trance-like state, because even though she had never heard the sound before, she knew it was regarding those two federal agents she tried to help earlier.

She checked her smart watch to see if she had missed any calls and saw that she had three messages awaiting her attention. Without even listening to them, she quickly came to the realization that they were going to need even more help getting out of whatever predicament they were in still mostly intact.

She took the express lift down to an underground tram system, which lead to, amongst other places, a landing pad with a workshop that housed a variety of craft from Rosen's impressive fleet. "In for a penny, in for a pound," she said aloud into the vacant tram car.

~

The four long, trying weeks since she agreed to look into Rosen for the DIA had culminated to this moment. Alena was inside their system, disrupting zone communications to aid in her associates' escape, while uploading the evidence Watson had procured onto their own streaming servers.

Despite all that, something didn't feel right. She had the nagging suspicion that she was missing something. She ran a quick diagnostic of her operations and there it was. Rosen technicians were naturally trying to shut her out, but doing so in a way she wasn't likely to detect until enough control had been regained to block and track her.

Alena noticed that they already had a foothold on the streaming financial and contract data, which wasn't as concerning at that moment as maintaining her zone communications link. She threw up a couple of virtual road blocks to slow them down, but it was only a matter of time before the much more experienced and well-paid software techs figured out how she was getting in through their back door.

Scanning zone security communications, she could undoubtedly see a spike in system processing activity. "The jig must be almost up," she muttered inside the seemingly empty situation room at the FBI field office on Kietzke Lane in Reno. Due to a lack of trusted DIA assets in the area, Agent Dune ensured her that she would be safe with the Bureau. It took some heated negotiations to allow her to use their computers unaccompanied, but once the Special Agent in Charge learned of why confidentiality and privacy were so important, he saw a promotion in his future and demanded to see what evidence she carried.

She redoubled her efforts in blocking the zones' automated defenses, but that would do little in the way of interfering with scrambling and coordinating manned security shuttles. She could see that three PT 109 short-range craft were already en route. With her role in this caper soon coming to an end, quite possibly in grandiose fashion, she hoped the others had a lucky charm of their own to put their faith into.

~

"Do you see them?" Hal asked anxiously, as he scurried around the porthole-sized windows of the medical bay cabin.

"Not yet, and stop asking!" Milo answered, his own angst raising with the other two's. "Trust me, when I see them, you'll be the first to know."

The triage medical extractor rocketed toward the nearest safe jurisdiction, which happened to be the state of Utah. This direction, unfortunately, was away from where they obtained the TME, as well as where Milo's Studebaker was parked. Upon realizing this, Milo recalled his car, but projected their current flight path and instructed it to intercept them by the most efficient route the onboard computer calculated.

The early afternoon sky was strikingly clear, and with the sun on their back, Milo was further allayed by the unobstructed view. Despite much of the state being utilized by the Rosen Games Network in one way or another, Nevada still retained much of its natural beauty. Even the striking Valley of Fire, with its red sands and picturesque rock formations, which could hypnotize people into thinking they had been transported to an alien world, could sway even the most stoic of individuals.

The former state park wouldn't get the chance to test its entrancing reputation this time however. What held Milo's attention were on the two gradually growing dark specks out of the forward view screen. A twinge of dread probed at his willpower. While he was confident they wouldn't be carrying any lethal ordinance, aside from perhaps a mounted machine gun, the cloud cars would most certainly have something that would knock them out of the sky.

"Our uninvited guests are finally about to make contact," Milo informed the others. Hal appeared behind him, with an oddly composed expression. "One coming from starboard as well," he added.

"I think, technically, *you're* the uninvited guests," Marcus corrected as he laboriously put on a clean shirt from a small storage cabinet labeled 'garment replacement.' "But I'm not sure they know that yet."

"Funny," Milo retorted. "Can you two secure yourselves to something? I suspect this is about to become a bumpy ride."

Marcus nodded and unfolded the two jump seats in the back compartment. TMEs were meant to *safely* carry a maximum of three people: pilot, medic, and patient. The brick red jump seats weren't very comfortable, a purposeful design choice so whomever sat on one wouldn't become negligent in their duties. However, the seats did offer a firm hold of their passenger with a five-point harness attached directly to the hull, and were positioned in a way where there was adequate views of both the medical equipment and at least one of the small windows.

The dots on the horizon were beginning to take shape. Milo could already perceive the slight downward curve of the delta-shaped wings. He also pictured the menacing, spiked nose piece as to avoid being intimidated by its overt fearsome motif. Milo wasn't sure if it was intentional, or merely coincidental, that the overall shape gave off an unassuming, even benign, look at a distance. To the untrained eye, it would often cause people to stop and stare curiously, due to its outline being unlike anything found in nature or made by man. He had heard comparisons of their silhouette to the Martian ships in the 1950 *War of the Worlds* movie. Up close and personal however, they told a different story entirely.

The craft approaching from starboard intercepted first, and swooshed past the view screen so closely it made Milo's foot hover over the air brake pedal. He knew right away that it was simply a scare tactic to encourage that exact response. Milo didn't fully fall for it, but the flyby gave him a better idea of what they had to contend with. The menacing, manta-like vessel, nicknamed the cloud car as an unshakeable joke, had virtually the maneuverability of a hummingbird, and could carry enough armaments to provide air support coverage for an entire division. The models currently harassing them looked to be stripped-down versions of their military counterparts; lessening their weight while increasing aerodynamics. The Rosen design also seemed to allow scary graphics to be painted on the dorsal and ventral sides, as well as replace the armaments with ion cannons.

"They're carrying buzz blasters," Milo yelled to the others. "We may be past the point for pleasant..." An explosion rocked the TME, or at least it felt like an explosion. "Is it too late to add that they may be carrying seismic mines as well?"

Ion cannons and seismic mines were both non-lethal weapons devised to incapacitate vehicles and power grids. Deionizing electronics causes circuits to fry and systems to shut down. Seismic mines use polaric-compression technology to simulate a highly condensed earthquake within a range of a few dozen meters, depending where it was constructed.

"Don't worry, they're just trying to spook us so that we stop on our own, and not have to ruin one of their likely *very* expensive vehicles."

"Well it's working!" Hal snapped. "At least the spooking part is. These jump seats aren't well insulated from shock waves. That blast made my teeth rattle like a ball bearing inside an old-style paint can!"

Milo didn't know how many of those mines the cloud cars carried, but their ship couldn't take many more hits like that. Luckily, it appeared they were changing strategies. Two of the patrol craft had taken up flanking positions off their port and starboard bow, with the third directly behind, lining up his cannons.

"Hang on!" Milo bellowed behind him, and then braced himself for the expectant crash they were about to experience.

Seconds melted by. Nothing was happening, so Milo let out the air he was holding in. When he did so, the cloud car to his right waivered violently, flipped over onto its back, then nose-dived into the sand and rock. There was little chance the pilot survived the impact at such speed, he supposed.

Another PT-109 patrol craft, with somewhat different markings along the hull, zoomed by, with the two initial aggressors in close pursuit. The newest arrival was leading them away from the TME, with the flying skills of an ace pilot. The aerial maneuvers were fast and fluid. The pursuers seemed completely outmatched, and the wavy, air warping energy of their ion cannons scattered wildly through the sky. One of the hostile cloud car pilots realized what was happening, or was told, and swerved around to regain its chase of the TME.

"What's happening out there? Can we relax now?" Hal asked from his jump seat, with strain in his voice.

"No! Keep holding on. In fact, hang even tight..."

Milo was cut short by a loud crackling sound, followed by the abrupt loss of almost all forward momentum. The transport skidded roughly to a halt, leaving a large swath along the ground. As the feeling in his arms and legs returned, due to the force his body endured from the seat restraints, Milo considered himself fortunate that they didn't flip over during the crash. Although he had never been in a vehicle that had been hit by ion cannons before, the incessant buzzing noise cued him in on where the name buzz blasters came from.

He unbuckled and trotted aft to check on the other two. They were found out of their seats, packing whatever they could into a couple medical bags, and Marcus's duffel.

"Leave the rifle and body armor too," Milo announced, catching them off guard. "They likely have tracking devices, plus they're a bit bulky and impractical to lug around."

Marcus stopped packing and gave him a dour look. "This is an H&K G11. Do you know how rare these things are? Well, the phase sevens anyway. The only versions that worked well enough to be adopted on a limited basis by NATO forces, and even the French Foreign Legion."

"Yeah, I do," Milo fired back. "Which is another reason why we can't take it with us. People would recognize it in a second. Now, if we've grabbed all we can and can still travel light, let's get moving. If our guardian angel out there covers us, my car can take us the rest of the way. It shouldn't be far."

The transition from the dark, smoky interior of the TME into the intense afternoon Nevada sun took some adjustment, but they quickly turned to traipse away from the relentless ball of fire. The air was dry and still, until a cloud car rocketed over their heads so close Milo thought he could reach up and touch it, if he wanted to. The craft made a wide arc to come around for another pass when something went wrong mid-turn. Its back end began a slow, vertical roll, as if its engines were tied to a string and was being pulled downwards. The y-axis rotation picked up speed, and the vessel smacked into a rocky protrusion hard enough to cause large chunks of it to slide away.

The reason for the second hostile patrol craft being knocked off their backs became evident seconds later. The final two cloud cars were engaged in a heated chase nearby. Milo figured either the allied craft got a shot off, or was somehow able to lure its pursuer into a situation where friendly fire did the job for them.

"We should try to do something to help," Marcus said. "The lead pilot is good, but it's only a matter of time before the other wears him down, or lands a lucky hit. Rosen doesn't hire just anybody. It's entirely possible that one, or both, are professionals, maybe even military."

"How do you suggest we lend assistance Airman, use harsh language?" Milo asked, still mesmerized by the dogfight overhead.

"I have a thought," Hal cut in. "But you're not going to like it." He told Milo his plan, and the man swore at him with such fervor, Hal couldn't help but laugh. "Is that the 'harsh language' you were referring to? Because it may be more effective than you think. I haven't heard some of those colorful metaphors since I was surrounded by Marines."

Still red in the face, Milo turned away from the other two and unfolded his tablet. He checked for the location of his car. The onboard tracking system indicated that it had passed ten kilometers and was closing. He looked to his left and could see it speeding toward him, like a well-trained dog running to its master coming home from a long day's work. He stared at it a moment longer and let out a heavy sigh.

"If I do this, and it works the way it's supposed to, will the DIA compensate me?"

Hal stared at the man. He was clearly distraught by the decision he was now committed to, so Hal had an obligation to try and assuage him in the most honest way he could. "I'll see what I can do."

"Yeah. That's what I thought," came Milo's flippant response. He sighed once more and activated his vehicle's manual controls. Velocity was increased to maximum, and he steered it directly toward the aerial acrobatics going on overhead. He was confident that if the lead craft hadn't spotted the Studebaker rapidly approaching, the vessel's proximity alarm had made its presence known. With this assumption in mind, he was growing nervous it wasn't veering off. In fact, it appeared to have increased speed!

"Uh, is your goal to take out *both* of them?" Hal asked with tension in his voice, obviously making the same assessment. Milo didn't respond. He was too focused on watching the sky, while steering from his tablet, waiting to make a split second maneuver.

The ion cannons of the trailing cloud car had finished their recharge cycle for the third time, so it resumed its attack. From where the three stood, it looked like the nearly invisible ionized energy was coming within a few dozen centimeters, and inching closer with each volley. The Stude was getting dangerously close as well. If there were anyone in the driver's seat of the car, they may have been visible by then. Milo really hoped they saw...

The friendly patrol craft took a sudden, steep dive, catching the following pilot completely by surprise. An ion blast intended for the other vehicle struck the Studebaker on the hood. The car began to drift downward, making it a larger target. Since the assaulting cloud car had increased speed to chase the friendly PT 109, there wasn't enough room to slow down or maneuver. It crashed into the Stude with such force that the luxury auto was bisected, and the three large pieces plummeted to the ground limply.

The last surviving patrol craft made one pass of the wreckage, and landed nearby. The two-section hatch opened like droopy eyelids. Who stepped out made two of the three men slouch in relief, but the third reached guardedly for his sidearm.

"Pick our jaws up from the dirt boys. Who else do you think it could've been to come to your rescue?" Sonya said with a cavalier attitude.

Hal and Milo exchanged conceding glances. Milo noticed Marcus's hand lingering over his pistol grip, like a cowboy in a showdown, and shook his head as subtly as he could. Hyde relaxed and uneasily readjusted the equipment bag strapped to his back.

"Well, it might've been less of a shock to us if you had answered your phone, negating the need to steal a Timmy," Hal rejoined jadedly.

"Yeah, I probably should've mentioned that I never answer my phone. Which is why I said *I'd* contact you, not the other way around. Anyway, as time is short, I should let you know that your scheme worked, or at least the part where Rosen's dirty little secrets were revealed, quite publicly. I'm here to clean up some of the mess you've caused in the interim."

"What does *that* mean exactly?" Milo asked suspiciously.

"I need to gather up the bodies, or survivors, of the three pilots sent after you and take them to the nearest med station, making it appear that I was there to help like the good colleague I am. I also should use some seismic mines on what's left of your car over there, to make it near impossible to identify and link back to you."

"So that's it? You make it sound like this won't get investigated at all," Hal said.

"Oh I'm sure it will be, but it'll be half-assed at best. They have more pressing matters going on right now than the loss of one man. Speaking of which, you should be clear of the zone communication inhibitors just beyond that ridge over there, so you can make whatever travel arrangements you need. Leave the bags though, the gun belt too kid. There'll be less of a demand to track you down if they're not concerned about stolen property on top everything else. Plus I might be able to use it to our advantage."

The three men exchanged nods, shrugged, and collected the bags into a small pile. "Ok. Anything else you want to bestow on us?" Milo asked.

"Yeah. Keep it in your pants until she's eighteen kid. Now, it's best you get moving so I can tidy up here, and work on my cover story."

"Do you really think that's going to work? Their surveillance systems *have* to be back up by now. Besides, it looks like you could use some help."

"They are, but we're in a sort of blind spot here. This area is never used for anything that would need to be watched. And don't worry about me. Like I keep trying to tell everyone, I can be very convincing when I have to be."

"If you say so. Good luck," Milo concluded as he turned to walk toward the ridge she indicated a moment ago; the other two in tow. Hal and Milo walked silently without looking back, but Marcus couldn't help but check over his shoulder every dozen paces or so. It occurred to him that he may have to get used to that practice for a while, until his name could be cleared.

Forever vigilant, in no small part due to his experience as Prisoner 74205.

Epilogue: Vindication

Chicago – Government Building, Dearborn Street

Milo sat at his desk within the US Marshal Field office, staring blankly at the back of his cubicle. It had been just over a week since the escape from Rosen's hunting ground, with the three men going their separate ways shortly thereafter.

While the Rosen Gaming Network was still a lucrative company, it had been neutered of its most popular and violent programs by placing a stoppage order pending investigation. As an act of contrition by some of the outed members of congress and other political affiliates, many of the zone properties had been annexed by the federal government and turned into wildlife sanctuaries. One of the most rapidly approved bills in US history.

Needless to say, acting like it was just another day after all he'd been through in the past ten days was a challenge. He'd received an award for his work on the Rubicon case. He tried to give it back, knowing all too well that Hyde didn't die in the zone as the official report stated, so he bit his tongue and drowned his conscience with some fifty-year-old bourbon he'd been saving for a special occasion.

To take his mind off all that, Milo was pleased to be assigned a new case the day before. It didn't receive a fancy code name, nor was he to be paired with an agent from outside the Marshals, but it was a sign that things were indeed getting back to normal. Then why was he so depressed about being back to work, he wondered?

Perhaps it was his new case; an escape from the recently reopened Joliet Correctional Center. Recognizing the old prison's notoriety in popular culture, a wealthy financier thought it a good idea to renovate the main prison, along with a few of its outbuildings. It was a rushed job, but somehow was able to reopen on its seventieth anniversary of closing in 2002.

It was widely known to those who follow the construction and conservation of prisons, that the

Alethea Foundation, which funds private detention facilities amongst other programs, cut corners at every turn. The escape of a man named Scofield however was so obviously an inside job that Milo wondered why it was still sitting on his desk. He stood up to ask his direct-line supervisor, Jamey Kirlan, that very question when he saw a familiar face weaving her way through the office maze.

"Good day Ms. Sarne. What brings you to my little piece of paradise? Or the more prudent question is, I suppose, *how* did you get in here?"

"Keeping promises Deputy Durron. And I have Justice Department credentials, in my real life that is. In case you've forgotten."

"Oh, right. So which promises are you referring to? I wasn't holding you to anything that I can recall."

"Not my word, not technically anyway, but Agent Dune's. Your last directive to us was to keep you on the same page, and to Harold that apparently still stands. Part of what Watson uncovered from Rosen was some of their... informants I'll say, for lack of a better term." She unclipped a data stick, disguised as a personal data transmitter, from a lanyard that hung around her neck. PDTs were used to track a person's whereabouts while they were at work or school. The devices were often integrated with employment or student identification cards, since those were typically necessary to have on hand for multiple reasons.

"This contains a list of names of individuals within the Department of Justice who had regular contact with Rosen in some way, until about a week ago of course." She stepped in closer and lowered her voice to a whisper. "One of those names is of someone who works in this very office. Seems he has a bit of a gambling problem and got mixed up in the Network's high risk bookmaker."

"That probably just described half the people in here, Can you tell me who it is, or do you want to keep me in suspense?"

"I haven't read the whole file, not my area of concern sorry to say, but the man's name is Kirlan..."

"That slimy rat bast... He's my supervisor. He personally selected me for the Rubicon case. I suppose this might explain how he was able to remain in Chicago for his temporary promotion, instead of getting shipped off to who knows where. Well, thanks. I'll have a look at this right away."

"There's still one more matter of business I'm to deliver to you Deputy Durron."

"Milo, please. Never mind the formality, and save yourself three syllables."

"Very well, Milo. My apologies. I don't warm up to people very quickly. Anyway, Hal wished he could be here in person, but he has already returned to his original mission. However, he didn't forget his promise to help you replace your beloved vehicle, that you nobly sacrificed I might add."

"No way. He was actually able to get me another one?"

"Not exactly. But it's the same year as your other one, and even the same color scheme."

"Ok. Where do I see this thing? Do I pick it up from some impound lot somewhere? Or will a friendly person posing as an insurance agent appear one day?"

"You can start by checking your parking space through the security feed on your desktop, which Hal wagered you became quite familiar with to watch over your previous car," she chided with a shy grin.

Without admitting that Hal had been right, Milo did as she suggested. After allowing the cameras to cycle through its series of feeds, he paused it as the image hovered over his assigned space. Although his wife had offered to let him use her car, he declined due to the efficiency of public transit in the downtown area. His parking spot had been vacant the whole week back, until now.

The frozen camera angle caused him to do a double take. The car's colors were strikingly similar to his Sky Hawk II. But upon further inspection, he had figured out what it was. "A Tesla Torpedo? It's a decent enough car, but probably about a third the amenities even the cheapest Studebaker offers."

"Hal assumed you'd say almost that exact phrase, so he's willing to take it back and see if something else comes along that's more to your 'delicate sensitivities,' as he crassly put it."

"No, no. I'm just giving you a hard time. It'll get me where I need to go just fine. Plus, it has an interesting story behind it, if you're ever inclined to check it out."

Much like its human namesake, Tesla Incorporated was forward thinking with their efficient, if not somewhat trendy, line of electric cars that helped to loosen the hold organizations like OPEC had on the world. In recent years however, they opted for a more classic, by-gone age look to house what soon became a standard engine.

One of those styles was modeled after the Tucker 48, of the short-lived Tucker Corporation. While the 48 was the official name of the vehicle, it was often referred to as the torpedo, and so the unofficial name was adopted into the Tesla line.

"I may just do that, but probably won't, full disclosure. So, unless there's something else, I bid you good luck, Milo."

"What will you do now?" he asked as she turned to leave in one, swift motion.

"The same as I always do; get on with my life, until my other life comes calling again. When that call comes, and I'm sure it will eventually, I try to be prepared. I suggest you do the same."

Milo watched her leave but said nothing, unsure of how to respond to her last statement. He scoffed, thinking it unlikely he would ever see her or Hal again, turning back to his desk, which contained a case he would probably solve by the end of the day. Then he looked at his new car projected onto the paper thin monitor and fantasized about what situations would make the call Alena spoke of present itself.

To be continued...

Acknowledgements

Inspiration has a way of springing up when you least suspect it. Like its predecessor, *Pieces of the Whole*, ideas for *Crossing Rubicon* came to me from various corners of my vast catalogue of useless trivia. Most of those sources are rather obscure, but parts of the main plot stemmed from a somewhat more recognizable novel known as *The Running Man* by Richard Bachman; a pseudonym of Steven King. I'm ashamed to admit that I had not come across this book until somewhat recently. Being a product of my time, I of course watched the film it was loosely based on. While I prefer the movie, surprisingly enough, there's something special about the book that wasn't captured within the screenplay, and I hope to have given it some justice here.

I once again thank my editor, Christel Hall, as well as another excellent cover design by Dafeenah Jameel at indiedesignz.com; I couldn't have done it without you! I'm also thankful for the many helpful and supportive people in my life. In large part, this book is for all of you.